Geoff Tristram has been  cartoonist for over thirty-five range of clients including Per Snooker, The BBC, Tarma , ..., Past Times, Ravensburger Puzzles, Reeves Paints, Winsor & Newton, Trivial Pursuit and the television show, 'They Think It's All Over!', to name but a few. He has created artwork featuring the likes of Jonathan Ross, Jeremy Clarkson, Ian Botham, David Vine, Steve Bull, Alan Shearer and Ayrton Senna, not to mention virtually every famous snooker player that ever lifted a cue. You may even have noticed him at the Crucible World Championships on TV, interviewing them as he drew their caricatures!

He has also illustrated many book covers, advertisements, album sleeves for bands such as *UB40*, *The Maisonettes* and *City Boy* (remember them?), and postage stamps, notably 'Charles and Diana – The Royal Wedding', 'Bermuda Miss World', 'Lake Placid Winter Olympics' and 'Spain 1982 World Cup Football'. More recently, his incredibly detailed 'Cat Conundrum', 'Best of British' and 'What If? jigsaws have enthralled and exasperated thousands of dedicated puzzle fans all over the world.

Geoff's younger brother, David, is a well known and extremely successful comedy playwright and film-maker, (check out the hilarious Doreen's Story and the Inspector Drake films on YouTube) so it was no real surprise when Geoff eventually turned his hand to comedy writing, hence this, his eleventh full-length novel; the third outing for his new comic creation, the chaotic and obsessive writer, Adam Eve.

Losing the Plot

Geoff Tristram

DRAWING
ROOM

First published in 2013 by The Drawing Room Press

Printed and bound by CPI Group (UK) Ltd, Croydon, CR0 4YY

ISBN 978-0-9926208-0-6

Cover illustration by Geoff Tristram. Who else?

Buy books online on www.geofftristram.co.uk or contact the author on gt@geofftristram.co.uk

After eleven novels, I suddenly realized that every plot I have ever devised is about some form of buried treasure. This is extremely odd! I have two possible explanations, which I will share with you, whether you wish me to or not.

The first is that, as a young boy living in a little council house in the Black Country, my lovely dad would tell me all about his favourite book and film, Treasure Island. This led me to love galleons, flintlock pistols, quill pens and hand-written, parchment treasure maps, and I still do.

Not that my stories have anything whatsoever to do with that era. Mine are all set in modern times, and are more to do with Ealing Comedies, TV farces such as Fawlty Towers, the convoluted plots of P.G. Wodehouse and the odd Jerome K. Jerome-like droll observation.

And yet.... the buried treasure is there every time, be it in the form of a painting, a map, a manuscript, a piece of antique silver, or whatever. And I swear, this has only just dawned on me. Our childhood experiences seem to stay with us all of our lives, don't they?

The second, and more prosaic explanation for this treasure obsession is that I have a very limited imagination, and I've just written the same book eleven times. I prefer not to dwell on this alternative for too long, for obvious reasons.

So there we are. Take your pick, but meanwhile, here is the third book in the Adam Eve series, and he's in sparkling form again. It's only 43,000 words, so it won't take much reading – ideal for the 21st Century attention span. Each hilariously funny chapter is but a bite-sized chunk, perfect for your tea break, but be warned. Gigglers beware! This book may be slim, but boy, it's potent.

GT.

Dedicated to my old friend Robert Williams, long-suffering Wolves supporter and Son of Halesowen, who somehow metamorphosed from talented young art student to copywriter, to Creative Director of Penguin Books, to scriptwriter for shows such as DCI Banks, Holby City and EastEnders. I may have been his hero once upon a time, but now he is mine.

In a few years' time I am fully expecting to hear that he has written several Hollywood Blockbusters, been made Prime Minister and become the first man to set foot on Mars. All this while somehow managing to remain one of the nicest chaps I know.

Oh yes - and any similarities that Rob shares with the fictional publisher Rob Wakefield in this story are entirely coincidental. My lawyer reminded me to mention that bit.

Chapter 1

The last sentence of my novel was finally completed. I had rewritten it at least twenty-seven times, and I was now satisfied that it was nigh-on perfect. I was more than satisfied – I was downright ecstatic, but my exhilaration very quickly turned to utter exhaustion and I flopped back lifelessly into the depths of my old settee, staring into space, too tired to move a muscle. Even my laptop seemed to breathe a sigh of relief. The small concluding sentence I was now mindlessly gawping at was the culmination of a whole year of blood, sweat and tears, and the mental relief of finishing it had suddenly reduced me to dried husk, a hollow shell and a spent force in the order named; a bit like one of those charred sky rocket carcasses you find poking out of your Rhododendron bush on November 6th.

A van passed by my living room window bearing the legend, 'Spratley & Son Ltd - Delivering Snack Solutions since 2003'. Ordinarily I would have found this amusing enough to laugh out loud. Now my bloodless lips could barely form a weak smile.

All writers believe that their work is special. Most are misguided – some much more than others on the

Misguided Writers' Richter Scale - ranging from the worthy-but-dull to the seriously loony. A very small percentage will actually write extremely good books, but even then, a publisher might not think them commercial enough, favouring instead something light and fluffy from the Romcom & Chicklit Academy (cue stifled yawn), which he knows will sell by the bucket-load to the Spanish Holiday Brigade. Sometimes you just can't win.

I am not, I readily admit, Shakespeare or Dickens; nor am I the new Steinbeck, Chandler, Jerome K. Jerome or Wodehouse – I'm not even Jeffrey Archer to be honest - but nevertheless, I was certain that this novel was a potential best-seller, and that publishers would be lining up to get my signature on their contracts. And yes, I can already imagine that superior, knowing look on your face as you conclude that here's yet another name to add to a very long list of deluded fools, but on this particular occasion you'd be wrong. You see, I'd already been informed that my book was, and I'm quoting here, 'very special indeed' (and not special as in 'special needs' either), and even more importantly, 'a potential best seller'. This comment, I should point out - before you assume that it emanated from the lips of my kindly but slightly biased old grandmother - was from someone who really knew what he was talking about. It was Rob Wakefield, no less, the Managing Director of Capybara, which is just about the hottest new publishing house in London. He had read all but the final chapter and was champing at the bit, impatient to wring the last few paragraphs from my over-heated quill, so that my 70,000 finely-honed words could jump to it and earn him a few bob.

Rob and I were old mates, you see – not that this would have influenced him in the slightest. As director of a big, thrusting, go-ahead outfit such as Capybara, he would be a foolish man indeed if he ever allowed his heart to rule his head. Even if his gorgeous, journalist wife had ever decided to write a novel and it fell below standard, she would stand absolutely no chance with him, so a casual acquaintance that he'd been at college with some fifteen years previously was way down the list. Rob was ruthless in business. He had to be. Capybara had a hard-earned reputation to uphold and a turkey could ruin that overnight. Obviously, I don't mean an actual turkey. That could probably ruin his swanky new office overnight, if it somehow accidentally became locked in there, but nothing more serious than that. I meant a literary turkey of course. The point being, Rob couldn't and wouldn't allow standards to slip. There were no favours granted, just because we went out to dinner once in a blue moon, or watched the occasional game of county cricket together, other than that he had promised me that he would read my story on the tube each day on his way to and from work. This kindly act - and I realize that I've just contradicted myself here - was in fact a *very* big favour in itself. You see, ordinarily, Capybara would never - repeat never - read unsolicited manuscripts. Authors have to find themselves a literary agent to represent them first, and these are even harder to land than publishers, which is saying something, I can tell you. Only a respected agent is allowed to present a manuscript to the big publishing houses, because this eliminates the illiterates, the loonies, the anoraks, the dullards, the dreamers and the odd psychopath, thus preventing them from wasting the publisher's precious time. The trouble is, virtually everyone thinks that they have a book inside them nowadays, but around ninety per cent of them should keep it there. Thanks to my connection, I had at least been spared this draconian screening process, but the favours stopped there, and I knew it. If Rob didn't care for my book, I was toast (and by that I allude to the cremated piece that's been dropped margarine-side down onto the filthy carpet of someone who owns a Husky dog with dandruff, and not the more appetising variety). Nor would he mince his words in telling me so. In fact, I reckon he rather enjoyed handing out bad news. That man threw compliments around as if they'd cost him a tenner each.

Impatient to hear his initial reaction, I had saved the novel onto my memory stick and got my local copy shop to print out everything but the last chapter, which I was still fine-tuning. The book was a comedy thriller, and had a complex plot with many strands that needed pulling together expertly at the end. I was finding the final chapter quite difficult to get exactly right, and I'd already rewritten it many times, so rather than show the notoriously critical Rob anything that was below standard, I elected to miss it out for the time being. I must admit that I also deemed this to be a rather clever ploy, in that, if he was intrigued by the story, he'd be on the phone to me, desperate to find out what happened at the end. I am such a tease!

I collected my copy of the manuscript from The Copy Shop, just a mile down the road from me, and posted it off to Capybara House, in the Strand, London (not far from Penguin's offices as it happens). I even paid a little extra to have it sent registered, though it grieves me to pay extra for a service that offers no more than the standard fee should rightly cover anyway. I digress here, but imagine going into your local corner shop, asking for a Mars Bar, and hearing the proprietor say:

"That will be fifty pence, (or whatever Mars Bars cost nowadays – I lose track) but if you want to make sure that it won't give you a dose of E Coli and kill you, or at the very least result in you being hooked up to a drip in hospital for two very unpleasant weeks, hallucinating and squirting liquid diarrhoea hither and thither, you can pay an extra pound, which will ensure that your Mars Bar is not only perfectly safe but more tasty than the standard version too."

Well of course, you'd look askance at the bloke and walk out wouldn't you? Mars, bless them, would never run a business that way. And yet this is what Royal Mail does to us on a daily basis and we meekly put up with it, just as we do when we enquire about the difference between first and second class stamps, if indeed there is one, apart from the cost. Anyway, all this aside, I forked out a considerable amount of money - seven quid if I remember rightly - to ensure that Rob had my manuscript in his well-manicured hands before 1p.m., in order that he'd be able to read it that evening on the tube if he so desired. I fully realized that another day stuck in the sorting sheds would have made no difference whatsoever; there was no deadline to worry about, and the package wasn't irreplaceable or even worth very much. Had it gone astray, I could have simply had another copy made for a few quid, but...well, I was excited and impatient. That's me, and I can't change the way I am. I make bulls at gates appear calm and contemplative.

Incidentally, you don't yet know anything about me, do you? Well, I'll take advantage of this temporary lull in the action to fill you in. My name is Adam, and don't laugh, my surname is Eve. Yes, I know it's a daft name, but I'm stuck with it. How I ended up with that sorry moniker is a long story which I won't bore you with now, but let's just say my parents weren't exactly brilliant at thinking of names for me or my siblings, Steven and Evelyn. Not that there's anything wrong with either of their names, *per se,* but it's what my folks paired them up with. They simply didn't think it through – the shortened form and so on.

So here I am, Adam Eve, a 38-year-old, divorced white bloke with slightly receding hair – okay, receding hair – and I've been told that I look a bit like the American actor, Nicholas Cage, for those who are partial to a bit of that physical description stuff that some authors go in for. Mind you, I've also been told that I look like the English actor, Robert Lindsay, and the much-loved comedian, Eric Sykes, as well, and I can't for the life of me see how you can look like all three at the same time. I'm sort of hoping that the Eric Sykes thing was more about my mannerisms, vocal delivery and sense of humour rather than physical appearance. Nothing against Eric of course, but it's not all that flattering to be compared to a deaf octogenarian comedian when you're only thirty-something.

I have two kids, Lauren and James, and an ex-wife, Katie, who I still get on reasonably well with, even though she managed to keep our substantial family home, while I had to start all over again. I now live all by myself - having recently lost my faithful canine companion, Len - in a small but pleasant end-of-terrace house in an equally pleasant backwater of a street, and that's all you really need to know for now. I don't know about you, but if I read too much of this descriptive stuff in one go I lose the will to live. I'll drip-feed it to you as we progress, but forgive me if I zip along. It's just that this tale is an absolute cracker and I need to get to what we writers call the hook - which arrives in the next chapter by the way - before you give up on me. Now where was I? Oh yes, well I'm a writer, as you must have guessed, which always sounds rather grand, but in my case, isn't, and I have a couple of fairly unsuccessful self-published novels under my belt, plus hundreds of whimsical magazine and newspaper articles to my name, though I'd have preferred to leave my name off most of them. We are not, I'm afraid, talking the Sunday Times here. At the moment I make ends almost meet by writing for those regional free newspapers that mainly consist of property sections, and those double-glazing ads that are always full of possessive apostrophes that shouldn't be there, and lacking those that should. If I'm really lucky, I get to interview a local TV weather girl or soap star that no-one's ever heard of for those County Life glossies which end up in doctor's waiting rooms alongside Yachting Monthly and those bizarre angling magazines that feature some moth-eaten character fondling a giant carp on the front cover.

I live - if you can call what I do living - in a town by the name of Stourbridge in the West Midlands which is, or at least was, famous for Robert Plant of Led Zeppelin, and glass-making, depending on what you're interested in. I'm surprised that they never thought of making glass busts of Robert to satisfy both types of tourist simultaneously. Maybe I'll suggest it to someone when I get a minute. I've always dreamed that I'd one day be the third reason for visiting the town, but currently my lack of fame is only matched by my lack of money. By my estimation, I'm still around a million pounds shy of being a millionaire, but I was hoping that the manuscript just about to land in the Strand would change all that. And as you already know, thanks to me flitting back and forth, it did, or at least, it promised to.

Rob rang me on the Tuesday to say that he'd received the story. He apologized for the brevity of his call, explaining that he was meeting a famous chef for lunch in Knightsbridge and a world-renowned rock star later that evening for cocktails and dinner at the Dorchester. Something to do with their autobiographies, he confided, which Capybara was currently pitching for. I accepted his apology, adding that I was busy and had to get off too. I had to purchase a tin of tuna chunks in Sunflower oil from Aldi before it closed. Oh yes, and the two-for-one freshly-squeezed orange juice, which is surprisingly good, considering. Rob asked me to be patient, adding that it could be weeks before he found time to read my effort. I assured him that I understood completely, but the voice inside my head was screaming, 'Read it RIGHT NOW you bastard - this bloody minute!'

I replaced the receiver and glanced over at a Capybara brochure which Rob had sent me some months before. I smiled one of my wry smiles when I realized that Capybara was only one division, or imprint, of the company, that specialized in thriller writing and, more recently, comedy, the new rock and roll. Ideal, as my novel was a comedy thriller! The reason I had afforded myself my wry smile was that the parent company, I discovered, was called Garden of Eden Books, and my name was Adam Eve. To me, this was an omen not to be ignored. We were made for each other – a marriage made in Heaven, as long as I didn't give in to temptation.

It was the following Friday when Rob rang me unexpectedly to say that he'd actually read my book, or at least all but the final chapter. As I stood in the kitchen, phone glued to my ear, I actually noticed my hand beginning to shake uncontrollably and felt my heart beating hard in my ribcage. I breathlessly grabbed a stool and sat down before I dropped, and I was already bracing myself for the dreaded word 'but', as in, 'It was okay but...'

The word never came. Instead, superlatives flowed out of the earpiece like Manuka honey, and from a man who seldom used them, to boot. For a mad second, I thought Rob had accidentally read Stephen Fry's manuscript instead of mine. That was it! Rob's P.A. had put the two novels in the wrong folders. Easily done! But no, it was definitely my book he was talking about, and he loved it. Or at least, he loved what he'd read so far. There was, after all, a chapter missing, but as Rob said, I'd have had to write completely inane gibberish in the last chapter to stop him from wanting to publish this book, and on the evidence of the rest of it, that was most unlikely. After adding something about how I'd finally come of age as a writer, after a thirty year adolescence, he concluded our chat by telling me that he wanted first refusal on the rights. If my heart had been pounding before, it was nothing compared to the Phil Collins drum solo it was performing when Rob mentioned the advance royalties. Unless his colleagues disagreed – and he couldn't see that happening, – I would be paid a whopping £50,000 upfront, which clearly showed how much they rated its chances. I was asked to sleep on it and maybe chat again the following day.

Somehow, I couldn't see me getting much sleep that evening. I watched a late night film to try and tire myself out, but I just couldn't concentrate on it, so finally I crawled up to bed at 12.30 a.m. I lay awake for what seemed like hours, chewing over the many aspects and potential consequences of what had happened to me. I was elated, confused and nervous in equal measure. And then, just before I finally managed to doze off, I heard the voice of my long-dead grandmother saying to me, "Adam, always remember, never count your chickens 'twixt cup and lip."

That woman made Mrs Malaprop look like Oscar Wilde, but even so, I knew exactly what she was getting at.

Chapter 2

I was sat bolt upright on one of Rob's posh leather chairs, trying to take it all in. All around me were framed photographs of writers that even I had heard of, looking suitably intense. One bloke had his index finger superglued to his cheek, with his thumb resting under his chin – the classic 'I'm an important writer' pose. Someone should have told him that we don't have to keep our heads that still anymore. It's not like in Dickens's time; these Nikon digitals have very fast shutter speeds nowadays. The truth was, I felt completely out of my depth, like I wasn't fit to shine their shoes. I felt sure that Rob would suddenly crack his face and say 'April Fool! You didn't *really* imagine we'd publish this piece of ludicrous puerile shit did you?'

Thankfully, he didn't do that. He asked if I wanted a cup of tea instead. I said 'yes please' to his young and achingly trendy assistant and after a brief exchange of pleasantries, she scurried off to arrange it. She was one of those girls that had a very bad case of Uni Accent, as I have christened it. She pronounced 'so good' as 'say gid' and everything she uttered sounded as if it were a question.

"I'll get you a couple of... biscuits?"

11

I knew what biscuits were.

"New Zealand Manuka honey and 75% organic dark chocolate chip. You'll love them, they're ...amazing?"

Was she really checking to see if I knew what amazing meant this time? I know I'm from Stourbridge and all, but surely...

Rob curtly waved her away and proceeded to get down to what we Brummies would call the *nittoi grittoi*. He was originally from that area, but you could no longer tell, whereas my accent, which I'd always regarded as barely discernable, now sounded very pronounced indeed in the rarefied atmosphere of the Strand. All I needed to complete the image was a flat cap, a packet of scratchings, a Woodbine and a whippet.

"Well," he beamed, "who'd have thought it? My old mate writing a sure-fire best-seller, eh? Congratulations are in order!"

"I'm still reeling," I admitted. "Do you really think it stands a chance?"

"I do indeed," said Rob, shoving my manuscript back across the table to me. I glanced down at it to check if it had the words 'Stephen Fry' scribbled anywhere on the cover, but it didn't. It was definitely mine. "So go away and finish it off, pronto, Tonto!' he grinned, adding, 'Oh, and is this your only copy, or can we hang onto it?"

"It's my only one at the moment," I explained, "but I'll get another one printed and post it to you if you need it for editing purposes or whatever; either that or I can send you a disc if you'd prefer it. I'd like to go through this copy on the train ride home if you don't mind. There are a few lines here and there that I want to tweak, and I want to have a bash at the ending while I'm in the mood."

"Feel free," replied Rob. "I haven't made a copy either. I was going to run one off here this afternoon to save you the time and money, but unfortunately our machines are being serviced at the moment so they're out of action for an hour or so. Still, a few days more won't hurt if you'd prefer to hang onto it. Just make sure you've backed it up. And one other thing, Adam. If you are *really* sure that we are the right publisher for you, and you still insist that you're not thinking of looking anywhere else, we'll get a contract drawn up as soon as the book's completed, so that we can sort out your advance. It's not mega-huge by our standards, I'll admit, but it's not too bad at all for an unheard-of writer. It's a reflection of the faith we have in this book of yours doing really well for us."

It may not have been huge to him, and I daresay that his famous chef and his famous rock star might have turned their cocaine-filled noses up at it, but to me it was wealth beyond the dreams of avarice, or whatever the expression is. I tried to not look too much like an over-excited spaniel puppy and retrieved my manuscript, promising him that it would be completed by the following week, if not earlier.

The adrenalin was really pumping now, and I was as jumpy as a hyperactive kangaroo on hot sand. I'd heard the door open and the pitter-patter of his assistant's Jimmy Choos, so I stood up rather quickly to help with the drinks. What happened next was a bit of a blur. I recall head-butting her silver tray from underneath with such force that

I thought I'd shattered all of my teeth, and I vaguely remember the sugar lumps cascading about my ears like cubist snow.

Shortly after that, my mind became a bit sketchy, but I eventually became aware that I was lying flat on the floor with my laptop miraculously still on top of my lap. Curiously, I was also convinced that my knees were on fire, but I put this down to the delirium caused by the blow to the head, which was now throbbing with much gusto. I raised a trembling hand to my brow to see if my skull had been cleft in twain, and as it passed by my eyes on the return journey, I noticed with some alarm that it was now spattered with a bright red sticky liquid that I instinctively knew was not Dulux 'Pillar-box' Weathershield Gloss, as featured on my new front door. Meanwhile, my knees continued to spontaneously combust, causing me quite considerable discomfort. Disembodied voices were enquiring as to my well-being; the answer to which, had I been fit and able to communicate, was 'significantly less than fair to middling, thank you!', but eventually the mists cleared to reveal Miss Moneypenny and Rob bending over me with looks of concern etched on their faces. Strangely, even in that state, I remember being mightily impressed with the young lady's ample cleavage, which was, unless I was very much mistaken, wobbling around unhampered by a brassiere, just in front of my battered and bloodied face. I couldn't be absolutely sure, but I think I saw one of her highly-recommended honey and chocolate biscuits nesting down there, looking enormously pleased with itself, if indeed biscuits can show emotion. I raised myself up with shaky arms to survey the accident scene, wiping my blood-stained right hand down my already tea-stained white shirt. A large brown industrial-sized teapot was lying upturned on top of my manuscript, which was to the immediate left of my scalded knees. Two bone china teacups with bold floral motifs were lying in pieces just under Rob's executive desk. I was surrounded by a fairy ring of sugar cubes, and a silver spoon poked out of my suit's top pocket at a jaunty angle.

"I don't usually like my tea to be as strong as that," I winced. I find it helps to defuse the situation, a touch of humour. Miss Moneypenny began to dab at my brow with a serviette. It stung like a serpent and I yelped, rather girlishly. Rob beckoned for her to back off and he helped me to my feet. Something told me that he endured, rather than enjoyed, her company.

"One lump or two?" he asked, his handsome, craggy features forming a half-smile. It was a good line, I had to admit. I wish I'd thought of it. One witty comment each, then. Fair enough; an honourable draw.

"I'm sooooo sorry!" said his assistant, holding her nose in place with her two hands, the way ladies do in times of emotional crisis, or while they're waiting to see if their answer was correct on a daytime game show. I thought for a moment she might cry, so I gave her as big a smile as I could muster. That's not so easy when your knees are throbbing from third degree burns. I looked down at my soggy manuscript with dismay. It had copped most of the half-gallon or so of boiling tea that had not ended up on my legs. It was, as our American cousins say, totalled. Had I not been a writer, but instead an artist, showing my latest unframed watercolour original to a swanky West End gallery, I would have been devastated, but all I'd actually lost was fifteen quid's worth of photocopying - nothing to a man with a huge advance heading his way. I waved it aside dismissively, as D'Artagnon might have done if he'd just been shown his execution warrant, signed and sealed by the King. I may even have nonchalantly flicked a bit of lint from my velvet sleeve as I did so, I can't remember offhand. It just meant that I would no longer be able to read my novel through again on the homeward train. No big deal. I had it on my laptop, after all. I'd probably be unfit to do any reading anyway due to the onset of concussion. Miss Moneypenny handed me serviettes to clean up my bloodied brow and wet, burnt knees. After a thorough examination, neither seemed potentially fatal. Meanwhile, Rob dabbed at his posh oak floor and retrieved the soggy script.

"No harm done," I grinned. "Trust me to do something like that at my big-deal publishing meeting. I must be the world's clumsiest man, I reckon. It wouldn't surprise me if I slipped on one of your soggy biscuits next, catapulted myself out of that open window, fell four storeys into the Strand and got squashed by a passing tour bus full of Chinese folks."

"Don't you bloody dare until you've finished that last chapter off!" frowned Rob. "After that, and maybe an even better sequel, you can do what you bloody well like."

I retrieved my thankfully unscathed new laptop and sat down again, nervously fingering my brow, which appeared to have almost stopped bleeding.

"It's okay," smiled Rob's assistant, "it's just a small nick. I'll go and get you a...plaster?"

She toddled off in search of the Capybara First Aid Box.

16

Rob asked if I was okay to continue, and I assured him that I was more or less *compos mentis* again. A severed leg wouldn't have stopped me from closing the deal on my £50,000, so a pounding headache and a vague notion that I was the Emperor Napoleon certainly wouldn't. Over the next ten minutes we dealt with a few legal issues, some of which I'd never even thought of. Rob asked who else knew about my novel, and I explained that no-one did, which surprised him. Call me eccentric if you will, but I usually like to write these things in isolation and I don't discuss plots with even my closest relatives. Ordinarily, I would never show friends and family a work in progress, no matter how impatient I was to do so, much preferring to hand over a *fait accompli* in published form at the end. I suppose it's similar to being an artist, and not letting anyone see your painting until it's finished. You don't want anyone criticizing something that's a work in progress, with the rough edges still visible. That said, I did break my own rule by sending the book to Rob with a few pages missing, which perfectly illustrates just how excited I was by it, I suppose. I just knew it was a bit special and I needed a second opinion right away from someone I trusted.

Actually, I think my reluctance to show anyone in my immediate circle of acquaintances springs from my early twenties, when I'd go to some party or other and inevitably get trapped in the corner of a squalid kitchen by a complete tosser who needed to tell me in great detail about the novel he was currently writing. Worse still, it was invariably a pretentious, nineteen-year-old marijuana-smoking hippy college kid who would bore me so rigid with his tale of underground kingdoms full of elves and warlocks that I would literally lose the will to live, and I meant the word

17

'literally' literally, before you start correcting me. My eyes would just glaze over, like those of a dead fish, and I could feel my life ebbing away, I swear. It is now my firm opinion that anyone under the age of twenty-five should be banned by law from trying to write a novel. Don't ask me why, I can't explain it in any coherent way, but it also brings to mind those horrible sixth formers who go in for politics. It's not natural. Kids that age should be out having fun, not smoking a pipe in the common room and reading books by Anthony Wedgwood-Benn, the bloody wankers. People don't have the necessary – what's the word I'm looking for – gravitas, that's it, until they get a bit older.

So no, I hadn't shown it to anyone apart from Rob. He breathed a sigh of relief and asked me to keep it under my hat for the time being, until the contracts were signed. He said it sounded all very cloak and dagger but there were good reasons for his caution. Things had gone wrong in the past. Ideas stolen, authors poached and so on. My grandmother's words echoed around my head once again.

"There's many a slip between chicken and lip."

I agreed to keep stumm until he gave me the all clear. Then I was going to shout it across the rooftops with a megaphone.

Business concluded, Rob emerged from his side of the desk and we shook hands. I gathered up my soggy manuscript and laptop and headed for the lifts, passing a still apologetic Miss Moneypenny *en route*. I pressed the G button, and the lift whooshed through four floors in around two seconds, turfing me out into the spacious marble-clad foyer where important-looking young executives whizzed past on their way to yet another meeting, or stood in clusters talking about where they should meet for lunch.

In spite of my wonderful news, I still couldn't help feeling like an impostor. The way to the front entrance was lined with even more framed photographs of literary greats, and they all seemed to be looking down their noses at me as I left. Then, suddenly, I was unceremoniously catapulted through the revolving doors and into the white light of a beautiful, early Spring afternoon, looking like a befuddled and disorientated meerkat. I finally got my bearings and headed for the nearest litter bin, which was fixed to a lamppost, just a few yards from the Capybara offices, but an extremely pungent tramp had arrived there just before me, and his needs were greater than mine. He rummaged around a bit, and eventually extricated a ham and cheese sandwich, I think it was, still in its plastic triangular packaging. The man's hands were as black as coal, but he didn't seem overly concerned about holding his sandwich with them. I watched, fascinated. A tramp in the Strand, mingling with the yuppies and executives, sharing their pavements and their sunshine – even sharing their Waitrose food. Fascinating! I just hoped the little green spots on the bread were pesto, and not penicillin.

I stood just a few feet away from this down-trodden gentleman, gazing this way and that, taking in the sights, sounds and, yes, the smells of London and trying not to feel belittled and overwhelmed by it all. It was high time I learnt to be more confident about my ability, I eventually concluded. After all, I was as good as the next man, as my dad always assured me, and I should never forget that. The only trouble was, the next man, geographically speaking at least, was a homeless tramp foraging in a bin for a mouldy,

19

maggot-ridden sandwich. I watched him shuffle away slowly and walked over to where the poor soul had been standing. He'd kindly left me a block of stale air to occupy – a tantalising mix of urine, sweat and cheap cider. I tore my sodden manuscript into a hundred pieces and deposited it in the bin quickly, before the stench got the better of me. I always loved visiting the capital, but I had to get home now. I had a novel to finish.

Chapter 3

I caught the Euston to Birmingham New Street train in the nick of time and staggered breathlessly through carriage after carriage looking for a spare seat, discounting ones that were next to very fat or sweaty people, borderline psychopaths, Glaswegian drunks and the folks who had strewn their belongings on the unoccupied seat to the side of them in a desperate attempt to ward off intruders. I eventually found a seat next to a young bloke with a neat beard who was engrossed in his laptop. He smiled pleasantly at me and gestured that the seat was free, and being a shrewd judge of character, our brief period of eye contact informed me that he was not going to knife me, bore me to death, or try to touch my bottom. I sat down, stood up again, removed my coat, slapping him in the face heavily with it as I did so, and reached over him to stow it away on the overhead luggage shelf. I sat myself down for the second time, and the middle-aged Indian couple opposite us promptly stood up with some urgency, jabbered away tetchily to each other in their native language and shot off the train at a rate of knots as it began to pull away.

This was a stroke of luck, as I hate sitting with my back to the engine and looking out of the window at where I've just come from. I stood up again (I think my fellow traveller tried his best to stifle a world-weary sigh at this point) and plonked myself opposite him now, mumbling an incoherent apology of sorts. His mood seemed to improve again when he realized that I'd only moved yet again in order to prevent him from feeling hemmed in and claustrophobic, and he rewarded me with a benign smile, before resuming his computer work. Then I stood up once more to rummage in my coat pocket, still situated above his head, for my extra strong mints which I'd left there by mistake, giving him a lovely close-up shot of my bare, hairy navel as I did so. I tucked my shirt back into my trousers, sat down again, and offered him a mint, by way of compensation. He refused, but not in an unpleasant way, and quickly got back to his work, no doubt rueing his decision not to drop his laptop bag on the empty seat when he first sat down, like all experienced rail travellers do.

We chugged along uneventfully after that, sharing no more than the occasional snippet of polite conversation, until he began to grow weary of his computer work around an hour into our journey. He removed his spectacles, rubbed his tired eyes and slipped lower into his seat, staring into space. Five minutes later, he was fast asleep. I had fully intended to attempt my final chapter whilst on the train, but somehow I didn't feel up to it. The meeting with Capybara had gone incredibly well if one excluded the part where Rob's secretary tried to batter my brains in with a tea tray and scald my legs with boiling water. Consequently, for much of the trip my mind was still racing, as I pondered the many ways that a successful novel would change my life forever. I was far too pumped up with adrenalin to write anything of merit for the first half of the trip, but now I suddenly felt mentally drained. I abandoned any thoughts of turning on my own laptop, and instead, decided to emulate my opposite number and get some shut-eye before the ugly, dirty monstrosity that is Birmingham New Street loomed large.

I must have been quite exhausted, because I don't remember anything after that until I woke with a start at Birmingham International. I don't know if you've ever done this, but my head suddenly slumped violently forward onto my chest as I slept, and I let out a startled yelp, which is always embarrassing in a silent railway carriage. I was still drugged with sleep, but I did notice my fellow passengers all looking at me and smirking. The train squealed, jerked and grunted to a halt, and a man with a strong Brummie accent said something or other on the tannoy system that was as unintelligible as it was inarticulate. As the mists cleared, I noticed the laptop man who had been sitting opposite me standing by the automatic doors waiting to depart. He caught my bloodshot eye and nodded. I waved back sleepily and began vigorously rubbing my tired eyes in an attempt to regain my focus. A thousand weary commuters leapt on as he leapt off, and once more the train lurched and juddered into action, en-route for the Second City. Fifteen minutes or so later, I made my excuses to the noisy Chinese family that had now surrounded me, grabbed my laptop and coat and staggered off the train, feeling as if some unseen hand had coated me in a thin layer of grime as I'd slept.

I made my way through the chaos that was the New Street rush hour, upwards on the creaking escalators towards the main thoroughfare and then I sought out platform 7b, where the Stourbridge train was due to make an appearance within minutes if the timetable was anything

23

to go by, which it wasn't. As I rode the down escalator to the trackside waiting area, downwind of a scruffy-looking bloke that had presumably just farted inside his donkey jacket and was too uncouth to care, I spied the filthy old diesel train just arriving, for once bang on time.

The train was packed with shattered, world-weary travellers desperate to get home to their depressing traditional semis, their starkly-lit living rooms with their lop-sided, cheaply-framed school photos that randomly break up the magnolia-coloured anaglypta walls, impatient to flop down into their worn old pink Draylon sofas to devour their sausage, egg and chips as they watched Coronation Street. God, I was jaded now. My only consolation was that the high flyers in their BMWs were still stuck in horrendous traffic jams on the M40, effing and blinding at the travel man on BBC Radio WM as he informed them that there was a serious accident at the junction with the M42 and all four lanes would be closed until the end of time.

I tumbled out of the train at Stourbridge and couldn't remember where I'd parked my battered old MG Roadster. I do this every bloody time I use public transport. I am in such a hurry to be on time for the train that I never think to make a mental note of my position on the car park. Never mind eh? Just a thousand or so vehicles to choose from, often in the dark, before I can locate mine and go home. Mind you, it could have been worse. After one disastrous visit to the Spring Fair at the National Exhibition Centre, I jumped on the courtesy bus and was asked by the driver, 'Which car park are you on, mate?'

24

Well, I did actually make a mental note on that occasion, but after eight hours at a show, I'd completely forgotten it. That, I find, is the trouble with mental notes. The chap tried to be helpful, as it was mid-winter and the snow had coated every car in the 12 square miles of car parks with a less-than-helpful layer of white, making them more or less identical to the naked eye. He pressed me on whether it was north, south, east or west, and I just stared at him blankly. Unwilling to give up right away, he pressed on gamely. He enquired as to the car park's number; was it, he asked, 1,2,3,4,5,6 or 7? He was met with the same dumb expression. I simply didn't have a clue.

As if the prospect of finding a white MG car hiding in one of 16 separate fields containing 22,000 other white vehicles in a snowstorm wasn't daunting enough, I was dressed in a thin summer suit and hypothermia was fast setting in. I was also, to cap it all, carrying a huge, heavy flight case full of books for reasons I won't bore you with. After much soul searching, I asked the man to deposit me back at the Atrium bar, where I nursed several cups of tea, making each last an hour, just like the poor old sod does in Ralph McTell's 'Streets of London' dirge, until the cleaning lady began to mop the floors and the manager politely asked me to leave so they could lock up for the night.

Mercifully, by then, almost all of the 22,000 white cars had gone home to their nice warm garages, and after a one and a half hour trudge through the tundra that would have taxed Scott or Amundsen, I eventually found my frozen sports car all alone in the farthest reaches of remote East 4, looking every bit as forlorn as I was. I have already spent far too long on this reminiscence, which is hardly serving to thrust the plot forwards, so I will not trouble you further with the tale of the flat battery, or the ridiculous cost of AA membership.

Anyway, to cut a long story short (and some would say it's far too late for that) I found my car after my Capybara trip with relative ease - thank the Lord - and ten minutes later I was back in my neat little Victorian end terrace, brain-dead but exceedingly happy with how things had gone, down in The Smoke. I poured myself a stiff Shiraz, threw together a simple pasta dish and watched some mindless TV for half an hour while I ate. After I'd chucked the saucepan, plate and cutlery into the sink to soak, I decided to quickly back up my novel onto a CD, just to be safe, before I called it a day. If I didn't, knowing my rotten luck, I'd wake up the following morning, ready and eager to begin my final chapter, only to find that my laptop had chosen that very night to commit suicide.

I took the machine out of its case and immediately something struck me. It wasn't my Laptop case. It was a subtly different design to mine – more expensive, I would have guessed. Even worse, it wasn't my laptop.

Chapter 4

I can't adequately explain to you how I felt at that precise moment. I just sat down and stared at the wall, while my mind ran the gamut of emotions from A to Z, and then back again. After what must have been twenty minutes of this strange mixture of mental anguish and physical paralysis I slowly emerged from under the ether with, rather surprisingly, a fairly positive attitude. The man on the train had obviously fallen asleep and realized that his stop, Birmingham International, had crept up on him and said 'Boo!' He'd then presumably woken up in a stupefied daze, as had I, and reached for the wrong laptop. It was a simple mistake, as the two machines were side by side and in similar bags. There was nothing malicious about his actions whatsoever. After all, he'd left me with his own computer, which was a better, more expensive model than mine, though, coincidentally, manufactured by the same company. The man would almost certainly now be in a similar state to me, panicking about getting his property back, along with all the irreplaceable stuff that was stored within it. He would surely be turning on my laptop any time soon, finding out who it belonged to and getting on the blower to me within minutes. That was if my computer held that kind of information. I couldn't for the life of me think if there was anything within it that would reveal my identity, let alone my address or phone number. I am so dumb when it comes to technology that I wasn't at all sure. Meanwhile, I opened *his* computer and turned it on while I gave that particular aspect further thought. It took the usual few minutes to warm up and then a panel opened up on the desktop. It asked me for my password.

Bollocks and bloody shit. I'd already hit a huge brick wall that I had no chance of climbing over. I did briefly toy with typing in random words in the vain hope that I might crack it, but after trying Beardy, Brummie, Rip van Winkle, Paul, Barry, Nick, Rhianna and Coldplay I gave up. It was a bloody stupid idea in the first place; I don't know what I was thinking of. I would simply have to be patient and wait for the chap to contact me. He'd looked a bit handy in a semi-nerdy, Bill Gates kind of way, so I was fairly confident that he could glean something from my Acer '*Aspire*' Model 5332 that would lead him to my door. Luckily, I'd never got round to sorting out a password for mine, so he wouldn't have the problem that I'd had, which was a blessing. And yes, bingo! All he had to do was to go into my emails and he'd find my address, and he could send me an email.

No he couldn't. I didn't have a computer any more. I used to have a PC in my little study until it went bump. I think it had received so many unsolicited adverts for Viagra and penis enlargement that it committed suicide. I replaced it with the new laptop, so everything of importance was stored on that. 70,000 word comedy novels, for example. I hadn't thought to back it up on disc. I never do, the reason being that I am a brain-dead technophobic cretin.

Thankfully, The Copy Shop would still have it on file, so I could pop round there the following day and get them to make me a back-up disc, while they were replacing my tea-sodden hard copy. Then I could at least write my final chapter while I waited for The International Laptop Thief to return the goods. This was comforting, of course, but I couldn't help but still feel a bit jittery about the situation I found myself in. It was getting late by now, but I didn't really want to crawl off to bed and lie awake fretting about it till four in the morning, as I was prone to do, so I took my wine glass back into the kitchen for a refill, thinking that this might help to relax my overactive mind. As I reached across the kitchen work surface to grab the bottle, I caught the stem of the glass on the edge of an open drawer – it was the lightest of taps – and the entire stem dropped off and shattered on my tiled floor. This pissed me off a good deal more than somewhat, as the goblet was a smart, reassuringly heavy, reasonably expensive cut glass affair made by Royal Brierley Crystal, which I won in a raffle at the cricket club. It was presented in a plush, purple, satin-lined box and I was very taken with it, and now it was ruined. To add insult to injury, the stem had shattered into around twenty-seven thousand pieces upon hitting the floor, and I had to spend the next ten minutes on my hands and knees rounding them all up, like a giant Welsh farmer looking for tiny little glass sheep. If you've never broken a glass on a tiled floor, you may not be aware of how far these bits travel. I am still finding them today on a regular basis.

Once I'd shaken the dust pan into the pedal bin and cursed again under my breath, I picked up the goblet and filled it with red wine, being as it was the only wine glass I possessed. I have to report that it was fine if I held it in my hand. I just couldn't put it down anywhere in between gulps.

The next morning I awoke at six with a raging thirst and a pounding head. To make matters worse, my tongue appeared to be stuck solidly to the roof of my mouth. I felt as if some unseen hand, possibly that of a keen cyclist, had applied a thin coat of contact adhesive from his puncture repair kit to both surfaces as I slept, allowed it to dry for ten minutes and then sat back with glee to watch the result. On reflection, however, I think it highly unlikely that this is what actually took place. I reached for my bedside beaker and drank the five-day-old half-pint of water that it contained in one go. I vowed, there and then, never to drink from a glass that couldn't be put down ever again. I crawled into the shower at eight and stood under the lovely, hot water groaning for ages until I felt equal to a spot of breakfast. The rhythm of my temples was like a heavy metal band's bass drum. I found that it fitted the beat of the Death March perfectly, a tune I hummed to myself as I boiled the kettle, in order to cheer myself up a bit.

The International Laptop Thief had not phoned, and with each leaden, depressing hour, the chances seemed less and less likely. Perhaps, I reasoned, he'd arrived home exhausted after a hard day in the humming metropolis, slung his computer down on the kitchen table and not even looked at it since. It being a Tuesday, he'd surely be heading back to the train station any time soon, and once he realized what had happened, he'd be in touch. It was after nine now, so I was going to give him until the arbitrary deadline of midday to contact me. It was no use panicking till then.

Midday came and went, and still no call. This meant one of three things. One: he hadn't gone to work and therefore he had not needed to look at his laptop. Two: he'd already spotted that he'd got the wrong machine but there was nothing within my computer that told him who or where I was. Three: He'd walked out of Birmingham International into the path of a Polish articulated lorry delivering very cheap cast-iron garden furniture to Poundland and been squashed liked a hedgehog, along with my computer.

To take my mind off things, I jumped into the trusty old MG Roadster and started her up. I was met with a satisfying throaty roar that was partly due to MG's proud heritage of sports car manufacturing, but mainly due to the huge hole in the exhaust pipe's silencer. I whizzed around the ring road, slowing down to 30 mph for every one of the several thousand speed cameras that they have installed there, threw a six to get off and exited in the direction of a smallish town by the name of Wordsley, where the Copy Shop was situated. I greeted the three members of staff that worked there, and in a moment of comedy magic, they all said 'Can I help you?' at exactly the same time, like an atonal barbershop quartet, only with one bloke missing, obviously. Still undecided as to which member of staff to address, I quickly discounted the large hirsute one with body odour, and also the gauche teenager with the artily untended monster hairdo that he was trying to hide his face behind, eventually plumping for their middle-aged, balding and bespectacled boss. Whenever I purchased photocopies or whatever, he always asked if I needed a bill, because if I did, he would go on to explain, he'd have to add VAT. The man would ask every person who used the shop the same question, as bold as brass, whether he knew them or not, like it was a completely above-board and legitimate

31

business practice. I'd love to have been a fly on the wall when the local VAT inspector popped by to get some copies done, one fateful day.

I asked the boss to knock me off two copies of the manuscript and two discs, just to be safe. He sat himself down at his computer and dug out my file.

'What's it called?' he asked.

''The Lost Sapper' by Adam Eve,' I replied. 'It's a comedy thriller about a sapper, who, erm, gets lost. It's very funny, as it happens. There's much more to it than that, obviously.'

'Was it saved as that?' he queried, adjusting his smeared spectacles, his garishly illuminated face set in a grimace of concentration, a few inches from the screen.

'Yes,' I confirmed, palms moistening just a little now.

'Col,' he called to the large hirsute, sweaty one, 'is Mr Eve's book on your computer, only it's not on mine.'

Colin sat down and messed around with his mouse. 'Yes, remind me; what's it called?' he asked.

'The Lost Sapper,' we sang in ragged two-part harmony, the boss in a rich baritone and me offering a rather dry soprano croak.

'Nah!' said Big Hairy. 'It *was* on here though, 'cause I did the copies the other day for him.'

He called over to the Gauche Thing, who was fiddling around with the colour copier up the corner, trying to look invisible.

'Justin, you don't know what's happened to Mr Eve's book do you? It was here the other day, I know it was.'

'What was it called?' asked the Gauche Thing almost inaudibly, moving a hairy curtain to one side and peeking out shyly from under it to show us his pimple collection. I was slowly losing the will to live now. The three of us told him at the same time. What was it about this place, I wondered. I'd heard of barbershop but never copyshop harmony before. I drummed my fingers nervously on the Formica worktop. The timid little teenaged mouse scurried over to the white Apple Mac and squinted at it.

'I think I, erm, accidentally wiped it,' he concluded, after a few seconds of painful silence. 'I thought it was finished with.'

Brian, for that was the boss's name, could see the anguish on my face at this point, and set about trying to reassure me before I could bite on the cyanide pill that I'd concealed in my hollow tooth for occasions such as this.

'Don't panic!' He said. He smiled weakly, before flashing his work experience boy a look that was meant to sting, 'we can retrieve it, no problem, can't we, Col?'

Col, the true techie of the trio (easily spotted as they are invariably fatter and sweatier than the others, and usually wear black T shirts with obscure heavy metal band logos emblazoned on the chest) concurred, explaining how this retrieval process was performed in far too much detail for my liking. He might as well have been speaking Serbo-Croatian or Esperanto for all the sense it made to a dimwit like me. After boring me to the very threshold of rigor mortis, he promised to look into it, as soon as he'd finished printing off five hundred full-colour leaflets for the estate agents who lived next door but one.

I breathed a huge sigh of relief, explaining how important this was to me, both spiritually and financially – but especially financially. They asked me to pop around at ten the following day and they'd have my job ready for me. I thanked them brokenly and left them to it. Brian escorted me to the door and hissed under his breath:

'If the little bastard concentrated on his work instead of his bloody mobile phone and his hairdo, and didn't feel the need to pop out the back every ten minutes for a bloody fag - a filthy habit that I am effectively financing, incidentally - he might have more chance of landing a proper job here one day.'

He apologized once more for my wasted trip and promised to give the young upstart a jolly good thrashing and me a discounted price. I hope it was that way round anyway. I assured him that everything was fine, as long as they weren't having me on about it being easy to find my deleted novel.

'Listen, Col might stink a bit and resemble a silverback gorilla,' Brian the boss grinned, 'but he's a flipping genius with computers, unlike me. I was a sales rep for a window company and I just bought the franchise. If he can't do it, it can't be done. We have ways and means, even if it's been deleted from the deleted items file and has now entered the abyss, so don't lose sleep over it.'

I left the shop feeling optimistic, but the loss of my laptop was still a worry. Surely by now, the chap should have realized that he'd picked up the wrong machine, unless, of course, he'd packed his bags and flown off on a two week holiday the next day. Knowing my luck, he'd probably embarked on a round the world cruise.

As I drove home after my wasted trip, I made a snap decision. I couldn't afford to hang around waiting for him to contact me. I had to be proactive and try to find *him*. He'd been on the train on Monday and got off at Birmingham International, so maybe he travelled to London each day to work. It was, after all, a rush hour train that he was on, so things looked promising in that respect. There was a Vermeer exhibition currently showing at the National Gallery which I wanted to see, so I could take a day off to go there, making sure that I caught the same train from Euston afterwards, trawl the carriages in search of him, and if that failed, hop off at International and hope he did too.

If he was nowhere to be seen on Wednesday, I would try again the following Monday, just in case he only used the train on Mondays, but this time I'd just drive to International and wait on the platform for him. If I still hadn't tracked the bugger down, I'd have to give up. After all, what if his London trip had been a one-off? Maybe he didn't work in the Big City at all, and he'd just been to see a client or a mate of his. I didn't mind taking a gamble and coughing up for a train ticket, but I wasn't made of money. Using the London train for a whole week was probably dearer than buying a new laptop anyway. I don't know how people afford it, I really don't!

So that was the plan. Two attempts, and then quit, or maybe I could try a last ditch appeal on local radio. At least my novel was safe, and that was the real concern. I rang The Copy Shop and told them I'd pick up my work the day after my London trip instead. With that huge publisher's advance making itself at home in my bank account, I could buy a hundred new laptops and still have loads of dosh left. I could have six laptops in every room, three in the lavatory, three in the loft and one or two in the garden shed for spares. I could have laptops beyond the dreams of avarice. If anyone popped in for tea, I could say, 'help yourself to a laptop' the way some folks would offer their guests a biscuit.

I drove to the railway station and bought myself a return ticket for the following day. I'd have done it online, but unfortunately I didn't have a laptop.

Chapter 5

I strode out of the National Gallery mid-afternoon on Wednesday, full to the brim with culture, spaghetti and meatballs. I'll also shamefully own up to knocking back several large glasses of Montepulciano D'Abruzzo, (try saying that when you've knocked back several large glasses of Montepulciano D'Abruzzo) even though I'd sworn, after The Monday Hangover, that I'd never drink again as long as I lived. Even fairly moderate drinkers like me have a knack of swearing oaths of abstinence in the morning, but curiously having no memory of that pledge come seven-thirty in the evening. Drinking during the day though, was truly unusual for me. Normally, I wouldn't thank you for the stuff until the sun had gone down, so I don't know what got into me. Maybe it was the stressful situation I found myself in, *vis-a-vis* the lost laptop and novel, or perhaps because the gallery visit had made me think I was on my holidays. Perhaps it was even seeing a Dutch cavalier in one of Vermeer's paintings getting a nice-looking glass of red down his neck which caused me to become the innocent victim of a subtle piece of 17th century auto-suggestion. Whatever the reason, I found myself stumbling down the first three steps and nearly breaking my neck once I'd left the building and the fresh air hit me.

I must say that they have an excellent little restaurant at the National Gallery, even if it has a tendency to attract intense, poncy, Guardian-reading London folks wearing white cord trousers, red sweaters and spectacles on chains around their necks. Anyway, the food was good, the wine was potent and old Vermeer was as brilliant as ever. I am quite the art lover, me, and have been since I was at grammar school. My old schoolmate, Dennis, reckoned I'd die of Vermeerial disease if I kept looking at all those Dutch paintings. Not a bad little joke for a spotty sixth form oik really, when you think about it. Sadly, he had to relinquish his promising comedy career when he became a left-wing councillor in Bradford.

Pleasure over, it was now time to get down to business. I couldn't face the tube at that time of day, with those foul blasts of hot, stale air blowing through the tunnels and all those tired, hollow-eyed, garlic-breathed, grimy commuters pressed up against me, so I splashed out and hailed myself a cab instead. As we began to fight our weary way through the traffic, my talkative cabbie and I, I spotted the Strand up ahead. It caused my knotted and combined locks to part, and each hair to stand on end, like quills on the fretful porpentine, if I may be permitted to quote the Bard of Avon for a moment.

That wonderful street had seen some life; that was for sure. I tried to imagine it as it must have been in the thirties, with all those debonair Burlington Berties promenading up and down in their white bowties, wing collars and silk scarves, heading for Simpson's to dine, or maybe to Piccadilly Circus in order to meet their sweetheart at the Eros statue. I next imagined how it would have been in the war years, with Vera Lynn singing her songs to keep everyone's spirits up during the black–outs and the air raids, and khaki-clad soldiers on leave with their girls, dancing the night away to Glenn Miller-style big bands. In my mind's eye, I saw red buses loaded with kind-hearted cockneys havin' a right old larf, and jolly, red-cheeked policemen wishing the revellers goodnight and shining their torches about in dark alleyways in search of stray Germans. It was all too marvellous for words. I don't think I've ever felt so soppy and sentimental about a place. And do you know what? I don't think it was just the lunchtime drink that caused me to slip on my rose-tinted specs. I'd grown up watching all those old black and white films with soft-focus actresses who spoke with posher accents than the Queen, and decent, upstanding men with their Trevor Howard and Jack Hawkins gravelly voices, wearing their snap-brim fedora hats and smoking Woodbine cigarettes. They would invariably be filmed in places like Piccadilly Circus, in a haze of atmospheric, monochrome pea soup fog, just like the one in 'Casablanca', at the airport. Call me a big old softy if you like, but the first time I ever emerged from the underground at Piccadilly and saw that iconic view, I nearly cried, it was so moving. All around me were the places I'd heard about as a naive little child living 130 miles north of London on a humble little council estate. Oxford Street, Regent's Park, Strand, Pall Mall, Buckingham Palace, Kensington, Knightsbridge... and being surrounded by it all was simply magical.

The taxi driver called to me in the back, worried that I'd 'gorn quiet all of a sudden, like', and I snapped out of my reverie. He wanted to know if it was my first time in London, and I replied, rather embarrassed, no, of course not.

'Oh, sorry, me old san,' he smiled. 'It's jast that, I jast glarnced at you in the rear-view mirror and you looked all sort of full of wonderment. Enraptured, like, like you was a 12- year-old kid at Christmas and you'd just seen Santa!'

We pulled into the Euston taxi rank with loads of time to spare. I paid him, adding a handsome tip that I couldn't afford, and made my way to the main concourse, which was packed with people arriving, departing, hugging, kissing, dossing, waiting, feeding, sleeping, hustling and bustling or just looking lost and exhausted. I studied the large departure board for a few seconds and then made my way to the correct platform. A scruffy young woman glided up from nowhere and asked me if I had spare change. I explained that it was impossible to know if it was spare at this relatively early stage of my life, and it was best for her to pop and see me just before I died. Only then would I have an accurate idea of how much loose change I had left and wouldn't be planning on using. She gave me a look that said, 'The sooner you die better as far as I'm concerned.' One day this sarcastic streak will indeed be the death of me, but I just can't help myself..

I sidestepped her before she knifed me, strode over to the news stand for some chewing gum and a copy of Private Eye, and walked briskly down the ramp to the waiting train. It must have only just arrived, judging by the many empty seats. I was spoilt for choice, but I decided to aim for the approximate section of train where I was sat two days earlier, just in case our friend was a creature of habit.

A long shot, I know, but I had to try everything I could think of to help this 100-to-1 flutter come up trumps.

Gradually, the train began to fill up, and I studied every new passenger carefully as they walked past me down the aisles. I am patently hopeless with names, I admit, but pretty good at faces, and so far, no one's fizzog was ringing a bell. That said, I wasn't really expecting to get lucky so early into the journey. It was at International that I had to be on my mettle. I needed to be the first off the train, so that I could position myself next to the escalators. The layout at that particular station is such that everyone leaving the train has to leave by that funnelled route. It is the only way out. If my man was on the train, I reckoned I had at least a 95% chance of spotting him there.

Bang on time, the station master blew his whistle and the 5.35pm London Euston to Birmingham New Street train lurched out of the station. I settled back in my seat with my copy of Private Eye and tried to read it, but the words wouldn't sink in. A young businessman who had taken the seat next to me answered his phone, and for the next twenty-odd minutes, he spoke really loudly to his girlfriend, making concentration even more difficult. Within a short space of time, I knew what he was having for his dinner, what Nick had said to Chloe, what Chloe had said back, and what Gaz in Marketing thought about that. I was kept informed about the sales figures for March (which were well down) and I now know all the gossip about what happened on Jerry's Stag Do in Edinburgh (he wore a floral dress and got arrested for pissing in a public litter bin, bless him).

41

I tetchily threw my magazine down onto the table and closed my eyes in a vain attempt to block him out, but there was something about the chap's bloody booming voice that dominated the entire carriage. Then, after what seemed like an eternity, he hung up and must have decided to visit the loo or the buffet car or something. I can't remember a blasted thing after that, until I suddenly heard the tannoy system say 'Birmingham', which woke me with a start. I grabbed my belongings, asked the annoying git next to me to shift, sharpish, and barged down the corridor to the automatic doors. The train squealed into the station (don't they ever think to spray WD40 on those wheels?) and the doors hissed open. I leapt off and ran over to find the 'up' escalator, my brain still addled with alcohol-induced sleep.

Only the escalator wasn't there.

I was standing on Platform 3 of Birmingham New Street. Birmingham International was twenty miles or so behind me. If the International Laptop Thief *had* been on the train, he was long gone by now. The air turned blue at that point, and it wasn't caused by fumes from the diesel train either. If I'd been wearing a hat, I would have taken it from my head, dropped it on the floor and stamped on it, the way Oliver Hardy often used to do with Stan's when Stan had disappointed him in some way.

What a bloody idiot I was. That was twice in one horrendous week that red wine had caused me a real problem. It really had to stop. I had spent £35 on a return ticket, £30 on a boozy lunch, £15 on a Vermeer ticket, £12 on a bloody taxi, a quid or more on Private Eye, and all for nothing. To add insult to injury, now I had to spend another

£20 on a taxi to bloody Birmingham International, where my bloody car was bloody parked.

An hour and a half later, I crawled into my house, grabbed the mail from the hall floor and dropped it onto my living room table, poured a glass of Shiraz into a teacup (yes, I know, shut up) and flopped down into my armchair, exhausted and extremely peed off. I picked up the mail again to see if anything interesting had arrived while I was out, and as I began to browse through it in half-hearted fashion, I realized that I could see my breath, it was so cold. This was odd, as the central heating should have kicked in by then. There was a leaflet from a local firm that wanted to replace my mahogany windows with white plastic ones, another from the local curry house offering me two for the price of one (excluding Saturdays), two utility bills, the Stourbridge News (urchin on front cover looking sad and pointing melodramatically to spot where his new bike used to be), and, what's this? A letter from Edgecliffe's Publishers!

Edgecliffe's Publishers were a very well-known, classy London company that had been around at least as long as Penguin. I knew the name well. They'd always come across as rather old school and staid. Respectable, if you like; a National Institution, whereas Capybara was more your young, new, adventurous, thrusting, brash type of outfit. Regardless of all this, I thought to myself, what on earth were they doing writing to someone like me? The answer was almost certainly something prosaic, such as a book club offer, judging by the address, which was headed with a rather disappointing 'To the Occupant' rather than my name, but I have to admit to experiencing a small frisson of excitement as I hurriedly opened the envelope.

Anything looks great after a gas bill, after all. Inside was a folded letter on crisp white Conqueror Laid (my favourite) bearing their distinctive logo at the top. There was also a photocopied sheet of text which I placed on the table for the time being.

It was a typed letter, again addressed non-specifically, to the owner of the house. It read:

Dear Sir or Madam,

We thought you would like to see the enclosed (See photocopy).

Edgecliffe's has recently published a book of letters, all written by the famous wartime writer and novelist, Thomas M. Bingham, of whom you may be aware. Bingham was a prolific letter writer, and corresponded with many well-known people during his brief but highly-prolific career, including the likes of Kipling, Churchill, and Agatha Christie.

The reason for writing to you is this. Several letters were written to his elder sister, Alison Bingham, and we have included them in the book because they were rather poignant, due to the fact that Bingham wrote them whilst imprisoned in a German concentration camp from 1942 to 1944. You will see from the enclosed photostat (taken directly from our new book, 'Drop Me a Line! – the Letters of Thomas Bingham'), that letters addressed to his sister, Alison, were addressed to 19 Enville Avenue, Stourbridge, which is, of course, your address!

We thought that you might find this interesting, if, of course, you weren't already aware that a very famous writer's sister used to live in your house during the war!

Sadly, Bingham died in the camp, publically executed by the Gestapo for trying to escape for the fifth time, and never got to see his beloved sister again, which makes their correspondence even more poignant. Miss Bingham remained unmarried and died in a nursing home at the age of eighty-seven, after suffering with Alzheimer's for several years. Thankfully, her carers had the presence of mind to send us a great pile of his letters when they were clearing out her things, and it was this thoughtful act that eventually gave us the idea of searching for more, which in turn led to us compiling this wonderful book.

Finally, if you would like a copy of the book, having discovered that you have a connection, we would be delighted to send you one, free of charge. Further copies can be purchased from all good bookshops at the cost of £25.99.

Best wishes,

Graham Bateman, Managing Director.

Well, this was most interesting. I had no idea. I took a quick look at the attached photocopy and my eye was immediately drawn to my address. It was very strange indeed seeing it printed on the page of a book, I have to say. I vowed to call on my next-door neighbour first thing in the morning and tell her about it. Old Barbara has lived there for nigh-on fifty years herself, so there was a possibility that she'd actually known this Alison Bingham lady. Absolutely fascinating! I intended to probe her

45

further, if you will excuse what sounded like a euphemism but wasn't meant to be. Barbara was a nice old lady, and loved a good gossip. Postmen, milkmen, window cleaners, newspaper delivery boys, you name it, all had to allow an extra fifty minutes onto their schedule because of Barbara. If anyone even paused outside of her house, she'd pounce from her porch like a spider ensnaring its prey, reel them in, quickly wrap them in knitting wool so that they couldn't escape and talk them to death. I'm just surprised that she hadn't already given me the low-down on the Bingham woman, during one of our many garden fence chats.

I was about to read the letter that Edgecliffe's had enclosed, but before I did so, I needed to address the heating problem. It was early Spring, and though the days were now getting warmer, the evenings were still very frosty sometimes, and I was freezing. I bounded upstairs to take a look at the boiler, and discovered that it wasn't working, and was not responding to bribery. I'd been having trouble with it for ages, and a plumber that I'd called out to fix in on a previous occasion suggested that I should get a new system, rather than keep throwing good money after bad on my dilapidated set-up. He *would* say that, I know, but he was right. Half of my radiators didn't work properly, some were rustier than the Titanic, one leaked quite badly, and the boiler wasn't man enough to warm up a Wendy House. It was time to bite the bullet and get a new system installed. I'd been putting it off because of the cost for a few years now, but with my book advance in the offing, I could at last afford to set the wheels in motion. I rang my mother, who was annoyed with me because she was trying to watch an old episode of Columbo. She is always watching either an old episode of Columbo, Murder She Wrote or Countdown. That, apparently, is all that older ladies do. In fact, it's actually quite difficult trying to ring her when she's *not* doing that. I've looked at my newspaper and I can't even find those programmes anywhere in the schedules. Maybe she has a very old TV, I don't know. Anyway, she gave me the number of her pet plumber, who she reckoned was very good, and 'reasonable', whatever that means. I then rang Paul Davis - for that was his name - completely forgetting that it was quite late in the evening, and my mother had always drilled it into me that one never rang people after half-eight in case they panicked and thought 'something was up'. When I lived at home, if the phone rang in the evening my dad would look startled and say, 'Who on earth can that be at this time of night?' whereupon my mother would start fretting and insist that she wasn't expecting anybody. My dad would then concur that he wasn't expecting anybody either, and add, 'I hope nothing's up!' and all the time neither of them answered the phone. Then, after around ten minutes of this headless chicken routine, my dad would finally pick up the receiver and ask nervously, 'Who is it, please?' with a curious strangulated sound to his voice, and after a pause, during which my mother tried to ascertain who it was by means of an elaborate and skittish charades sequence, with my dad shooshing her at regular intervals, he'd eventually say something along the lines of, 'Oh, it's only Eric from work. He needs to borrow my socket spanners. You frightened me to death, Eric, I thought something was up.'

Paul Davis answered the phone, and I apologized profusely for ringing at nine-thirty.

'That's alright', he replied. 'I was just watching a crap old episode of Columbo, and I thought there was something up. How can I help you?'

I explained about the boiler, and how I was freezing, and he said I'd rung at exactly the right time. Mrs Noke's husband had passed away unexpectedly, at the age of ninety, and she'd had to cancel her job, which was scheduled for the following morning. He'd been due to put in a brand new system, and had put all the stuff in his van ready to make an early start when she rang him, sounding very upset. He'd offered his condolences and was resigned to taking it all back to the trade centre, but if my needs were similar to Mrs Noke's, I could have it instead.

Well, this was a stroke of luck for both parties, if not the third one, so I booked him there and then, and I couldn't help thinking that if I'd followed my mother's advice and not rung him after the watershed, the plumber and I would both have been the poorer for it. Apparently, the old lady's bungalow and my terraced house were roughly comparable in size, and a quick whizz round the house with my tape measure confirmed that most if not all of the radiators would be perfect too. Paul would be ringing my doorbell at nine the following morning, and he expected the kettle to be whistling at five past. That was another few thousand quid swallowed up. It was shaping up to be the most expensive and disastrous day I'd ever had, and I was beginning to wonder what else could go horribly wrong for me before I went to bed. I chucked my tape measure back in the kitchen drawer and sat down on the settee with my cup of Shiraz and the free paper. Lord knows why I bothered to read the thing, as there was never anything in it except men holding giant cheques for charity, hammy photos advertising the latest amateur dramatics production and little girls in karate outfits kicking out at the photographer with what appeared to be a giant foot. I skimmed over the cover story, turned the page and glanced at page 3, where a large headline caught my eye. It read:

WORDSLEY PRINT SHOP BURNS DOWN.
Work experience student's cigarette blamed.

Chapter 6

To say I had a sleepless night would technically be a lie. I must have drifted off for an hour or so round about half-five, I guess. Until then, my mind was in a state of turmoil, as I tried to get my head around the myriad possible ramifications of what had happened. Now I was well and truly in the mire, unless of course the International Laptop Thief suddenly materialized, which was looking ever less likely. I could have tried contacting the owner of The Copy Shop, but I didn't really want to add to his considerable list of problems the day after his world, not to mention his roof, had fallen in. I imagined him sitting in a sad, bare room somewhere, smouldering gently - and I mean that quite literally, not metaphorically - his eyebrows charred, his shoulders heaving up and down as he sobbed brokenly. Now was surely not the right time to ring him (presuming his phone hadn't melted), and ask, 'Where's my bloody job?'

Besides, there was no point whatsoever if the newspaper photographs were anything to go by. The place was razed to the ground and I was now officially in the mire. In spite of this, I couldn't resist a dry, sardonic smile, when I remembered Rob Wakefield's wise words about backing up my work and burning a disc or two, just to be on the safe side. The Copy Shop had done that alright, but the discs weren't so much burnt as bloody cremated. My only chance now was to make contact with the man on the train by whatever means, even if that involved a newspaper and radio campaign. I wasn't about to let my dream of becoming a best-selling novelist turn into a nightmare without a fight. I eventually decided that I would stick to my original plan, and drive over to Birmingham International Railway Station that evening. If that failed, I'd think about a Plan B then.

I somehow managed to shower and dress myself on automatic pilot, and staggered downstairs, ready for the arrival of Paul the Plumber. Still restless and agitated as a result of the catastrophic news, I opened my front door and ventured out into the street, where I spotted the plumber's van a few yards to the left of my house, parked half on the pavement with the back doors open. Two radiators were already propped against the far side of my wall, so I lugged one down the entry to help the man out, and returned for the other, larger one. The van was unoccupied, with everything just as the driver had left it, a bit like a plumber's van version of the Marie Celeste. This was odd. Then I noticed the man in the overall, chatting to my next door neighbour, Barbara, at her front door, and all became clear. She had seized her moment and collared him before he could start work. I smiled a wry, knowing smile, picked up the heavy radiator and struggled down the entry with it. It looked as if I now had time for a spot of breakfast, as Barbara's chats seldom lasted less than fifteen minutes, with some lasting well over an hour.

No sooner had I poured the milk onto the cornflakes, the front doorbell rang. I opened the door, and there stood Paul the Plumber, a pleasant, slim forty-something that put me in mind of what's-his-name, the chap from the Carry On films. It'll come to me in a minute.

'You got away light!' I grinned, welcoming him in.

This appeared to take him into dark and unfathomable waters. He smiled, but in a nonplussed kind of way.

'Barbara next door,' I explained. 'She could talk for the British team, that woman.'

'Oh, right,' replied Paul, somewhat non-commitally. Jim Dale, that's his name. The chap from the Carry On films, I mean.

I made my excuses, as my cornflakes were getting soggy, and left Paul to bring in his tools and the rest of Widow Noke's unwanted central heating system.

After I'd finished breakfast, we toured the house looking at radiators, and I showed Paul where the old boiler was situated. He explained that his usual partner for more involved jobs, such as this one, was busy elsewhere for a day or two, but would join him as soon as possible. The work was likely to take several days, during which time there would be major disruption, noise, doors left open all over the place and floorboards removed. In short, not the ideal place for a writer to finish the final chapter of his novel. I nodded resignedly; I had feared as much. Mind you, currently, it wasn't as great a problem as it might have been because I hadn't, at that sorry juncture, got an unfinished novel to finish.

I made Paul a cup of tea, and decided that it was best to get from under his feet. I handed him a spare key, telling him to let himself in and out as he wished. My mother always spoke highly of him, assuring me that he was completely trustworthy, and her word was good enough for me. Besides, I think you can just tell with some people, don't you? I grabbed my coat and told him I was going to buy a newspaper. Ever the optimist, I was hoping that the newspaper would dramatically reveal that The Copy Shop that had burnt down in Wordsley was not the one I frequented, but another one of the same name. I left the house and turned right towards the shops. Paul had now pulled his van down closer to my house, and several more radiators were leant up against my wall, plus a large cardboard box that I took to be my new boiler. The lady across the road, who is one of those Neighbourhood Watch busy-bodies and a seasoned Curtain Twitcher, gave me a filthy look, though for what reason I had absolutely no idea.

I purchased my newspaper and quickly scanned it for more information about the demise of The Copy Shop, but there was none. To clear my head, which felt as if it contained around a thousand writhing maggots, I decided to walk the long way round the block. I had not got very far when I spotted an A4 poster taped to a lamppost, asking for information on a missing cat by the name of Puddles. I presumed that the owner had christened it Puddles because of problems with house training, but this was merely speculation on my part. The poster included a photograph of Puddles, and I have to say that it was a peculiar looking creature; dirty brown, black and singed-looking in spots, like it had been trapped in The Copy Shop when the fire took hold. Still, I'm sure that its owner loved it, and that was all that mattered. I walked on, and blow me down, if this self-same feline didn't jump out of a bush and wind its way around my ankles, purring seductively. I bent down to examine the charred-looking feline and look for a collar, and like virtually every other cat, it didn't have one. I stroked the little thing, which seemed to go down well, and after gaining its confidence, it allowed me to pick it up. I held onto it with one hand and with the other, felt for my pen and policeman's notebook, which I religiously carry about my person, just in case I get a rare flash of inspiration. I made a note of the owner's name and number, and then, abandoning my walk, trotted back home with my new friend. Paul had brought in the boiler now, and a huge toolbox, leaving me very little room to manoeuvre in my cramped hallway. I gingerly negotiated the obstacle course and made for the kitchen, to a backdrop of bangs and creaks that were emanating from the bathroom area. I don't know about you, but I love the sounds of industry, especially when I'm not involved in it. It makes me feel as if things are happening; moving along, if you know what I mean. Poor old Puddles looked ravenous. I poured some milk into a dish and opened a tin of tuna chunks in sunflower oil that I'd earmarked for my lunch, and she – I sort of presumed it was a she anyway, though I didn't like to look – wolfed the lot down in seconds. I was interrupted at this point by a loud knock at the door, which was open anyway, thanks to Paul. Plumbers, incidentally, if you don't already know this, always leave every door of your house wide open, whatever the weather. I mention this just in case you were in two minds as to whether to engage one. I struggled back through the obstacle course and standing there, looking rather stern, was a police officer. On spotting me, he enquired, 'Mr Eve, is it?' and I answered in the affirmative, with a slightly apprehensive smile.

'Do you mind if I come in for a moment, sir?' he asked, and I said, 'If you can get in', or some such tosh. Not very inspired or original I'm afraid. I can't be witty all of the time. It would over-tax my brain.

We carefully made our way to the living room, and I invited him to sit down, which he did. I was beginning to panic a little now, as his grave expression suggested to me that something was seriously wrong, and I don't know about you, but, plagued as I am with a vivid imagination, I always convince myself that it's going to be about a very close relative that's been flattened by a ten-ton truck. I think he could see that I'd gone sort of anaemic-looking and a bit giddy, so he began by assuring me that no one had been hurt, which at least put my mind at rest a little.

'We've had a report from a reliable source', he began, 'that you have been seen stealing someone else's property. Can you enlighten me, Mr Eve? Is this true?'

'WHAT?' I replied, incredulously, and reddening a little. 'I've never stolen anything in my life! Who on earth would accuse me of that, for goodness sake?'

'I see you're having some work done, Mr Eve,' he continued. This policeman was not only misinformed about my being a part-time burglar, but he also had a butterfly mind and could change topic at the drop of a hat.

'Yes, I'm having a new central heating system installed,' I said, not having a clue where this was leading, if indeed it was leading anywhere.

'Very expensive business,' he smiled, empathetically.

I was just about to say something along the lines of, 'Sorry officer, but I'm rather busy,' when I remembered all those old episodes of Columbo that my mother watched. Whenever anyone said that to the detective, you knew right away that they were guilty. I bit my lip. 'Yes, it is expensive,' I said, and left it at that.

'And is that why you stole the radiators, Mr Eve?' he continued.

'Stole the radiators?' I queried, my voice rising to an exasperated squeak.

'From outside, in the street'.

'You can't steal your own radiators, officer,' I laughed. 'Has this come from that mad old bat opposite, by any chance?'

'No, Mr Eve, well yes, but essentially no.'

I gave the officer a withering look. I thought I saw his face colour slightly, and he seemed to be struggling to articulate his thoughts.

'The complaint has come from...'

We were interrupted by a loud knock on the front door. I hopped over Paul's assault course again and found yet another burly beat bobby blocking out the light.

'Come in,' I smiled, 'your colleague is already here.'

He went flying over the toolbox and bashed his helmet on the living room door. It was a good job that he was wearing it – the helmet, I mean, not my door. It would have come sharp otherwise. The door, I mean now, not his helmet.

It soon became apparent that they didn't even know each other and were calling for completely different reasons. I have seen less farcical episodes of Fawlty Towers. I asked which one wished to continue; I was easy. Eventually, the new chap had a go.

'I am here to ask you about a missing cat,' he said sternly. The original copper eyed me suspiciously, as a mongoose would a snake.

'God! That was quick', I said, stunned. 'I haven't reported it yet.'

'Have *you* lost a cat as well?' asked the second copper, puzzled now.

'No, I've found one,' I explained. 'Just a few seconds ago, in Bridle Road.'

'*Found* is an interesting way of putting it,' said the second copper sarcastically. 'I would suggest that a better word would be *stole.*'

'Ah,' smiled the first copper. 'So not only do you steal other people's radiators, but you steal cats as well. Quite the little Artful Dodger aren't we, Mr Eve?'

Paul the Plumber popped his head around the door at this juncture, and seeing that I had company, was about to withdraw, when the first copper invited him to add his two-pennyworth.

'Sorry to interrupt when you're busy, Adam,' Paul said, 'but I need to ask you a quick question about your radiators.'

'So do we,' said the first copper.

'You know I said on the phone that you might just need two more...'

The two coppers gave each other knowing looks.

'Well, I'll pop to Wickes tomorrow and buy a couple, shall I?'

'No need,' said the first copper. 'He's just stolen a couple and hidden them up his entry, haven't you, Mr Eve? The Neighbourhood Watch lady across the road saw you take them while Mr Edwards was distracted by Barbara.'

'Who the hell is Mr Edwards?' I asked, frustrated beyond belief. I get very confused when I watch films and they introduce too many characters all at once. I even struggled with Robinson Crusoe.

'Mr Edwards is the plumber working at Barbara's next-door neighbours,' explained copper number one, referring to his notebook. I did think I could break the ice by telling him that I had one just like it, but it didn't seem like the right time.

'For Christ's sake, I AM Barbara's next door neighbour,' I said, 'and the plumber is named Paul, and he knows about the bloody radiators down the entry.'

'I don't,' said Paul.

Puddles the cat chose this moment to wander into the living room, meowing for attention.

'Is this *your* cat, sir?' asked copper number two. I actually felt a fuse or two blow in my head, I swear. I took a deep breath through my nose and closed my eyes for a moment. Then I launched into it.

'Attention folks. Let me have a run at this without interruption please. Just listen for a while, if you could. Right, I have just helped carry two radiators round the back for my plumber, Paul, see Exhibit A, standing there, holding a red tea mug. It now appears that they were probably not, in fact, Paul's radiators after all, but presumably those belonging to another plumber, a Mr

58

Edwards, Exhibit B, who must have left them propped against my wall, before he got distracted by Barbara, or Exhibit C, who is my next-door neighbour. He, Mr Edwards I mean, must be doing something or other with two radiators at her other neighbour's house. I haven't got a clue what she's called. Let's call her Mrs Bird-Table, or maybe Exhibit D if you prefer. I erroneously – nice word lads, look it up – took the radiators thinking I was helping Paul the Plumber, or Exhibit A, over there, when in fact I was actually nicking off with Mrs Bird-Table's ones, under the watchful, if jaundiced eye of Mrs Curtain Twitcher over the road. As to the cat, Exhibit - where am I up to? E, I think - trying to be the model citizen, and seeing a poster about a missing cat called Cuddles, or Puddles, or some damn thing, I then rather fortuitously spotted said feline and rescued it, allowing it to wine and dine at my expense before I contacted the rightful owner, Exhibit F. That's where you came in, Officer Number Two.'

'Can I butt in?' asked Paul the Plumber, who had briefly disappeared but had now returned, looking troubled.

'Not yet, please,' said the second copper. 'I have just had a call from Mrs Miles, who has been sticking up posters all over town asking for information on her lost cat, Puddles, as you rightly say. She was looking out of her bedroom window just now, when she saw you, Mr Eve, bend down and entice her other cat, Widdle - Puddles' sister as it happens – into your arms and then abscond with it. She dashed out and followed you round the estate into Enville Road, and saw you disappear into your house with the creature. She was very upset, as you can imagine, after so recently losing the first one.'

59

'Erm, excuse me, folks,' said Paul the Plumber, with some urgency now. 'While you've all been sorting this out, the scrap metal lorry has only been and taken three of your new radiators, Adam. I'm ever so sorry, mate. I thought they'd be okay for a minute or two, propped up against your front garden wall. I ran over the road to ask that nosy woman if she'd seen who was responsible, but she says she didn't see or hear a thing!'

Chapter 7

I have never been so happy to vacate my house, I can tell you. By the time we'd sorted that lot out, it was time to drive off to Birmingham International. I couldn't believe my luck, I really couldn't. I seemed to have become some form of human chaos magnet. After a disastrous, not to mention expensive day in the Big City, followed by the extortionate cost of a new central heating system and the dire news that potentially my last copy of 'The Lost Sapper' had been incinerated, I was now down to the tune of three large new double radiators and a tin of Aldi tuna chunks in sunflower oil. To add to this, my reputation as an honest, upstanding pillar of the community was in tatters, and it was now only a matter of time before the good folk of Stourbridge started wagging their fingers at me in the street and shouting, 'Behold, the Cat Burglar and Radiator Thief!'

I screeched onto the huge Birmingham International car park, grabbed a parking ticket (more expense) and ran over to the escalator that ferried passengers to the main ticket office and waiting area. I scanned the information boards and dashed down the steps to the platform, just as the tannoy announced the arrival of the 7.00pm train from Euston. Gasping for breath and doubled up with stitch (which I always thought only affected junior school children), I staggered over to the doors by the 'up' escalator, offered a silent prayer to whomever it is that's up there looking after us – almost certainly no-one in my case – and fixed my eyes on the train that was about to come to a halt in front of me. Suddenly, twenty or so doors opened simultaneously and passengers started to flood out, all walking briskly in my direction. So far, no one looked anything like my man. The initial tsunami of commuters soon reduced to a trickle, and I was just about to give up and grab a cup of tea from the cafe upstairs, so I'd have something to cry into, when I saw the station master or guard, or whatever he's called nowadays, helping a passenger off the train. The chap was struggling to deal with a briefcase, an overcoat and two crutches, and he didn't appear to be winning the battle. I walked forward to get a better view, and I have to report that the poor man looked as if he'd had an argument with a mad bull and come off second best. His cheek was grazed and scabbed over, there was a band aid above his eyebrow, and his spectacles seemed to be held together with masking tape. He thanked his helper, who waltzed off in the other direction, and then he slowly began to hobble his way towards the escalator, like a city businessman version of Long John Silver but without the parrot. I stepped up to him and introduced myself as the chap who'd inadvertently taken his laptop, even though it was in fact he who had inadvertently taken mine. I thought it wise not to burden him with anything else, as he looked as if he'd got enough to contend with.

His face registered recognition, and he smiled weakly, exposing a broken front tooth. He tried to shake my hand, but it was a foolhardy act, given that he was hanging onto two crutches. I suggested that I should help him with his load, and, if he had the time, we could spend five minutes sorting things out in the cafe upstairs.

We sat down in a secluded corner and I fetched us a pot of tea for two. He seemed eager to explain what had happened, and why he'd not been in touch, but before I sat back to listen, I handed him his laptop, and he breathed an enormous sigh of relief. Apparently, it had irreplaceable work on it, to do with his job at an architects' firm in Holborn. I knew exactly how he felt. He took the computer from me and stroked it lovingly. Then his facial expression changed from that of a Delighted Laptop Recipient to Severely Depressed Harbinger of Doom, as he began to explain what had happened to him on that fateful Monday evening. It was quite clear to me that just having to recant his experiences one more time for my benefit was causing him untold mental anguish.

'I'm very sorry that I haven't been in touch,' he began, 'but as you can see, I've been somewhat indisposed. I got off at International on Monday night, as you know, and like an idiot, I grabbed your laptop bag instead of mine, because I was half asleep and in a rush. If you'd have been awake, you'd probably have spotted it, but you were zonked out as well.'

He took a sip of the boiling tea with shaky hand and continued. Most of it ended up in his crotch (I felt more than qualified to empathize) or in the saucer.

'Anyway, I made my way to my car, which was at the far end, bloody miles away from the station. It was pretty dark and miserable and the car was covered in frost, (this man was indeed a kindred spirit!) so I put your laptop on the roof for a second and started to scrape the windscreen with

63

my credit card. The next thing I know, some bloke, dressed in black, snatches your laptop off the roof and tries to leg it. I ran after him and grabbed hold of his coat, and he swings round and whacks me one right in the face. It was freezing cold, which doesn't help, and I'd got this bloody great overcoat on, so I wasn't quite Amir Khan in terms of agility, if you know what I mean. It bloody hurt, and I saw stars, but I tried to punch him back, and then all hell broke loose. He swung the laptop bag at me and smacked me right in the mouth with it, and I heard my tooth go.'

I didn't like where this was going. Now it was my turn to attempt a fortifying gulp of tea, and I have to report that my hand was no steadier than his had been. I'm sure I could actually hear the whooshing sound of fifty grand flushing down the lavatory. I became dizzy, and for a second I saw two Long John Silvers in front of me, doing the Twist. I reluctantly begged him to continue.

'I fell to the floor in agony,' said Jeremy – I'd asked him his name as we ascended the escalator - 'but this didn't seem to be enough for this bloody sadist. He started putting the boot in and ranting at me in a strong Belfast-type accent, stamping on me, punching me, he was like a rabid animal. Physically, I was much taller, but he was one of those small, stocky, shaven-headed thugs like you see at football matches sometimes, the psychopathic skinhead pit-bull type. I didn't know what had hit me. I ended up curled up in the foetal position, praying for it to stop before he killed me. When it was clear that I was no longer a threat, he helped himself to my wallet, my car keys and your laptop. He nicked my car as well, and left me for bloody dead in the far corner of the freezing cold car park. I was too badly hurt to drag myself off the ground, but luckily a lady had seen what happened and she got help for me. I spent the night in hospital, but thankfully he didn't do me any permanent damage. They said I could thank my big heavy overcoat for that. I'm very sorry about your computer, Adam,' he concluded, 'but hopefully there was nothing too important on it, and you can get one to replace it on the insurance.'

I sighed a heavy sigh and drained my bitter cup. So that was me knackered then. I had pretty much exhausted all avenues now. Suddenly, I felt incredibly selfish for thinking such a thing, when this poor lad had been through hell. I buried my own feelings and asked him what the police were doing about it. He said that the officers who had come to his assistance were appalled by the level of violence this psychopath had shown. They reckoned that he probably had a drug dependency and would do anything to feed it. Apparently, they were so concerned that this monster was at large, they have decided to include a reconstruction of the incident on the next episode of Crimewatch.

'Oh really?' I asked. 'And who have they earmarked to play you? Brad Pitt maybe?'

Jeremy smiled a sad smile, exposing the gap where his tooth used to be.

'More like Cess Pitt at the moment,' he laughed, before wincing with pain. 'It's my bruised ribs,' he said, 'it hurts when I laugh; the old cliché. Thankfully, there's not much that's making me laugh at the moment. Look, I really appreciate all the effort you've made to get this back to me. Here's my card if you need me to talk to any insurance people for you. The computer is probably long gone now, sold in the pub for twenty-five quid. Oh yes, and here's the number of the police station dealing with it. They gave me

65

a crime number, but it's an unusual situation when you think about it, because it's a crime against you as well as me.'

I jotted the information down in my policeman's notebook, and we shook hands. I helped him down to the taxi rank and saw him off, the poor sod. I walked over to a litter bin that was minding its own business and kicked it so hard that I thought I'd need crutches too. Then I looked up to the heavens and screamed:

'Just once, just fucking once, you bastard, could you not just let me win one?'

A big, homely-looking Jamaican lady covered her young son's ears up and gave me the look of death, before scurrying off in the opposite direction, making me feel deeply ashamed and miserable. I paid for my parking, jumped into my old MG and drove home.

Chapter 8

Paul the Plumber had taken over my house, and now his mate Pete had arrived and brought more radiators with him, making the place even more congested. I sat, dejected, on my old settee and took a closer look at the photocopy that Edgecliffe's had kindly sent me. It read:

Miss Alison Bingham,

19 Enville Road,

Stourbridge,

Worcestershire,

England.

My dearest darling favourite sister Alison,

In fact, my only sister so you'll have to do! Thank you so much for your letter, which cheered me up most wonderfully. I hope life in suburban Stourbridge is not too traumatic, or dull, for that matter, and that no more of Herr Hitler's bombs have found their way to your little backwater. I read your last about the big devil that failed to go off when it landed on the Liberal Club billiard table. I

67

couldn't help but smile. I bet that was the best cure for constipation those two old blokes playing billiards have ever experienced. On a sadder note, I have just been informed that my London home has been demolished during the Blitzkrieg. I am heartbroken, as it was full of the loveliest oil paintings, the ill-gotten gains from my successes as a writer. I still live in fear that I shall be found out and exposed as the creator of unspeakable tosh. Maybe this is God's way of punishing me for all those terrible books that I have written! Mind you, Edgecliffe's inform me that 'A Dream of White Cliffs' has just topped 40,000, and that during a war too, so I must be doing something right I suppose.

Say hello to the folks for me, and tell them chin up. Things have begun to get sticky around here but I don't want them or you worrying about me. My own fault really. Jerry keeps insisting that I remain here and be a good boy, and I keep insisting that I'd rather be somewhere else, thank you very much. I'm afraid that I'm failing to amuse them with my impersonation of a giant, Eton-educated mole, and they have begun to tire of my behaviour more than somewhat, bless their hearts. I won't go into the gory details, but that's about the size of it, my sweet.

Lord knows if this package will ever reach you. Everything is on a wing and a prayer nowadays, but the Red Cross do their best, albeit after Jerry has gone through everything with a fine-toothed comb, making sure there's no cake with a file in it, not that you'd need a file in Stourbridge! Thankfully, there is a German guard here who seems a decent chap, and he helps as much as he dares to. He read several of my books just before the war, he tells me, so they can't be all bad (the Germans, not the books, I mean).

68

Thanks you for the warm socks. I have sent you some stuff for safe keeping. Look after it till I get home, would you?

All my love, and don't keep worrying about me. I'll be fine!

Love to all, Your Tom.

I wiped a tear from the corner of my eye and dropped the photocopy onto the coffee table. There was something about the stiff upper-lipped wartime style that choked me up; that and the fact that I already knew the outcome.

Here I was, kicking innocent litter bins up in the air and upsetting nice, God-fearing Jamaican ladies because I'd lost a manuscript, while this man was calmly writing a last letter to a beloved sister, with the shadow of the execution post looming over him. In fact, the more I thought about it, the more the strange coincidences and parallel situations presented themselves, and I'm afraid that they didn't show me in the kindest light. This man was a writer too, but a successful one. His world, like mine, had been turned upside down by circumstances beyond his control, and his career had been cruelly and unceremoniously cancelled. I was feeling hard done to because of a lost book and a house that was in a bit of an untidy state, but he was somehow managing to remain stoic after his London home, full of his precious belongings, had been wiped from the face of the earth. Add to that the loss of his freedom, and the very real chance that he knew he could soon be facing a firing squad, and the only possible verdict was that he was a selfless hero and I was a self-absorbed worm. All of a sudden, this letter from Edgecliffe's seemed fortuitous. It had arrived in order to help me see what a shallow git I was becoming. I recalled my initial reaction upon hearing poor Jeremy's story. I felt very sorry for myself, because he'd managed to lose my laptop. Feeling concerned about him being beaten senseless came a poor second, a minute or so later. I know it sounds a bit daft, but I really do believe that things happen for a reason, as if some unseen hand is guiding me through life. There have been so many strange coincidences, so many things that have initially gone wrong, only to lead to better long-term solutions, that I am starting to question whether I have a guardian angel looking out for me. Some call it Karma, I believe. I don't have a word for it, other than spooky. Somehow, this letter had arrived bang on cue, and for some reason, it had inspired me to get off my arse, rise to the challenge and triumph over adversity. The next time I found myself feeling sorry for myself, I'd think of Thomas M. Bingham, robbed of his career, his family, his home, his freedom and eventually his life. I made a cup of tea and began to think positively. First, I rang the policeman in charge of Jeremy's assault. He thanked me for getting in touch, and explained that he already knew the laptop did not belong to the victim. He promised to get in touch if and when anything came up, and informed me that the television programme, Crimewatch, was scheduled for broadcast in two weeks time. The producers, he explained, were currently casting the look-alike actors, and as soon as that was sorted out, a reconstruction would be staged and filmed in the Birmingham International car park. I couldn't resist asking the officer why Crimewatch's look-alike victims were always far better looking than the real thing, and he replied, 'That's show business, my friend!'

Next I rang the managing director of Edgecliffe's, Graham Bateman, on his personal line, and thanked him profusely for the kind gesture. I took advantage of the free book offer, but also ordered several more for presents. I daresay old Graham knew I wouldn't be able to resist doing that, the crafty old sod. Talk about Vanity Publishing!

I did have another very important call to make, but I simply couldn't face it. I needed to ring Rob Wakefield and explain to him that my potentially bestselling novel was lost forever. It would be one hell of a traumatic phone call, and I was dreading it, not least because I knew he'd hit the roof. Like a complete buffoon, I hadn't backed up my work, and by so not doing, I'd not only lost myself £50,000, but I'd also lost Rob a damned sight more. I couldn't imagine him being all sweetness and light, somehow. There was another reason that I was stalling, however. If the police caught Jeremy's attacker, he might, just might, spill the beans on who had the laptop, if of course he'd managed to shift it yet. It was one hell of a long shot, but worth stalling for.

Rob had given me a week or two to complete the novel, so I decided to wait until he rang me. After all, sometimes it is wisest to do absolutely nothing. Once, by way of illustrating the wisdom of this philosophy, I was invited to a casino evening at some dull corporate event or other, and we were all given two hundred pounds worth of tokens to spend. It wasn't real money; this was just a silly game. The winner at the end of the night was the one who'd made the most profit. Personally, I can live with or without casinos, so I pocketed the tokens, forgot all about them, and chatted to a barman all evening instead. Meanwhile, everyone else but me was playing the wheel and chucking their fake money around with gay abandon. When the game ended at

71

midnight, we all had to count up our winnings, and the one who'd accrued the most pretend money won a crate of Champagne. And guess who won it? Yes, me, of course, and I did so by not playing. Everyone else had given most, if not all of their money to the croupier.

I therefore decided to bury my head in the sand and let Rob phone me. Quite what I'd say to him when he rang, I didn't know. In my quieter moments, maybe in the wee small hours, I intended to ponder that one. Meanwhile, I wracked my brains to see if there was any possible way of retrieving my lost book, short of actually rewriting it. I read recently that a very famous writer actually lost all of his manuscripts on a train, and was forced to start all over again. I can't for the life of me think who it was, offhand, but I really couldn't entertain that notion. I'd worry that all my replacement sentences mightn't have been as good as the original ones, and I think it would be a recipe for insanity. If only I hadn't torn the tea-soaked manuscript to bits and thrown it in that bin in the Strand. Hindsight is a wonderful thing, is it not? I heard a story once about a man and his friend driving a car around Berlin in 1934. As they round a sharp bend, a young chap, who is in a world of his own, walks right in front of the car and is flattened. The two gents jump out of the car to see if the poor fellow is okay, and mercifully, he has only slightly injured his leg. They pick him up and dust him off, and the daydreaming victim says 'No real harm done' and limps away rubbing his sore leg. As the two friends drive on, one says, 'Do you know who that was, Stefan? He's an up-and-coming young politician by the name of Adolf Hitler. Thank goodness you didn't kill the silly bugger!'

I made Paul and Pete the Plumbers a pot of tea and asked how they were getting on. The new boiler was now *in situ*, and they'd placed the old one at the front of the house with a sign attached which read:

Please feel free to steal anything you like without asking, just like you did yesterday, you shitbags.

I found this dryly amusing. I didn't realize that Paul was such a wit. He informed me that they would soon be moving operations downstairs, so that they could begin screwing the radiators down before the bastards took all those as well. The phone rang, so I dashed into the bedroom to get the extension. It was Rob Wakefield. Oh Jesus Christ! He asked how I was, and followed this with a preamble about how he'd just come back from watching his little lad playing cricket at school. This bought me precious time to work out what I was going to say, so I let him do all the talking, while I restricted my involvement to one word answers and the odd laugh, and all the time my mind was working at a million miles per hour and simultaneously my anal sphincter was becoming pretty much air-tight. I was like the oft-quoted graceful swan with its legs going like the clappers beneath the water, only if its legs were going at half the rate that my brain was, it would have shot down the bloody river like a speedboat. I could sense that Rob's opening gambit was about to wrap up at any second, and I knew damn well what was coming next, so, quick as a flash, I decided that it was best to come clean and tell the truth.

'Anyway, enough about my bloody boring domestic life,' Rob laughed, 'so how's the last chapter coming on?

'Erm, well, I've had a bit of a hiccup, Rob,' I spluttered. 'I've, erm, broken my wrists.'

Chapter 9

'You've broken your wrists, *plural*?'

'Er, yes, I'm in agony. I can't even, erm, wipe my own arse.'

'And how, prithee, did this happen?' he asked, a tad tetchier now, I thought.

I couldn't answer him. I hadn't had time to think that bit through yet. Rob's tale about his son's cricket match was over too quickly. I maintained an undignified silence and manically scanned the room for inspiration.

'I said, how did it happen? You still there?'

'Oh, yeah, sorry, you cut off for a second there. I, er, fell over a central heating radiator at the top of my stairs. I put my hands out to break my fall and it broke my wrists instead. I can't type, can't eat. I'm living on soup. It's a nightmare.'

'So who's holding the phone?' asked Rob.

'Er, I've got, erm, Paul with me, the plumber.'

'Bloody hell, Adam. Bloody hell. You are a bloody cretin, honestly. So what's the prognosis? When can I have my book finished?'

Rob was sounding a bit narked. I suppose these Big City publishers are under a lot of pressure, with deadlines and so on. Meanwhile, I was desperately trying to remember what having a broken wrist entailed; how one's hand would look, whether the fingers were still able to wiggle about freely and grasp things or tap at computer keys, what the recovery time was likely to be. Why on earth had I suddenly decided to come up with such a daft lie at the last second?

'Sorry, Rob,' I interrupted, 'I've just got back from the hospital and I'm a bit shaky and sick. I suppose it's the shock setting in. Do you mind if I ring you back tomorrow when I've had a rest, and I'll fill you in properly. Don't worry though; I'll get round it somehow, even if I have to dictate it to a secretary.'

I put the phone down.

What a twat I was. What an absolute brainless twat! I had spun him a lie that had bought me more time, and then, just as I'm home and dry, with my very last sentence, I suddenly come up with a solution to my imaginary problem, which means that I can complete the book quickly after all. Me and my big mouth. Why couldn't I have just shut up after the bit about feeling unwell? I always go a sentence too far. I must have been dropped on my blasted head as a child. The trouble with me is, I tell such good lies that I end up believing them. I was desperately trying to find a way of finishing a book with two broken wrists, and I cracked it. Whoopee! Hire a secretary, genius! The next thing you know, I'll be attempting to sue Paul for leaving the radiator at the top of the stairs and causing the accident. I swear I don't know what's real and what's made up any more. I was losing the plot mentally, due to the fact that I had lost the plot physically. How's that for a cracker?

I bit the bullet and rang Rob back right away.

'Er, look, Rob,' I said, trembling like a leaf, 'You know I just told you I'd broken both my wrists?'

'Yes.'

'Well, I, erm, look, it was a lie.'

'I see. Excellent! Adam, mate, I haven't got time for silly games. I have a large company to run and I'm trying my best to make you well off in the process. What's bothering you?'

'Sorry, Rob, this is very difficult for me...'

'The truth this time please. I'm all grown up now. I can take it.'

'I'm, er, having a bit of trouble with my nerves. A bit of depression. I've got writer's block as well. I can't seem to string three words together.'

'Jesus, mate, it's only a small chapter. It's not 'War and Peace'. I have to say, I'm a bit disappointed. More than a bit actually.'

'Cheers!'

'No, no, I'm not unsympathetic if it's genuine depression. I'm not inhumane, but you presumably know how to end the thing. Your book I meant, not your life, for God's sake.'

'Yeah! It's just...'

'So how does it end? We can get someone to finish it for you. It'll be good, seamless. No one will ever know.'

I stared at the ceiling and cringed.

'No, no, I...I just couldn't allow someone to finish my book for me, Rob. It's just not ethical. Look, I'm not in a bloody padded cell or anything. Not wearing a straitjacket and eating with plastic cutlery. It's just a bit of depression. The doc says I'll be as right as rain when the little pills kick in. I think it was brought on by the stress and excitement of it all. Suddenly, it dawned on me that I had a potential best seller, and my nerve went. You know those cartoon characters that run off the end of a cliff, and their legs are spinning round, and it's only when they look down and realize that the ground's gone from under them that they suddenly fall like a sack of spuds? Well that's me. Look, Rob, please don't lose faith in me, I beg you. We're old mates, and I won't let you down. Please, can you put this on hold for just two months, maximum, and I promise to deliver your book, perfect and on time. That's all I ask.'

There was a silence that seemed, to my scrambled mind at least, to be making a hell of a lot of white noise and lasting about an hour.

'Right,' said Rob eventually. He was sounding very terse indeed now. 'Here's the deal, Adam. In precisely two month's time, I will ring you again, and you will say to me, "I have the finished manuscript here in my hand, and it is brilliant. I am bringing it to London right now." Subject to the ending not being utter gibberish, everything will be as it was, and we will proceed. If, however, you do *not* say this, I will reluctantly have to wash my hands of you and move on. Is that clear? Have I been fair to you?'

'More than,' I tried to say, but my throat was so dry that I uttered no more than a parched gulp. I tried again and just about got the words out this time.

'Two months,' repeated Rob, and banged the receiver down on me so forcibly that I leapt out of my seat like a rocketing pheasant. He did not sound like a happy little Capybara, it has to be said.

I stared at the wall, my mouth open like that of a trout that has just been bonked forcibly on the brow with a fisherman's priest. When I finally came out of the ether I began to curse myself with a passion, petulantly kicking my small metal pedal bin across the room, and leaving it with a large, unsightly dent. What was it with me and defenceless waste bins, I wondered. Each time Rob and I had spoken, I had intended to tell the truth, but on both occasions, inexplicably, I had changed my mind at the very last second. I knew why I was doing so, naturally. I was stalling for time in the vain hope that my lost novel would turn up. It was understandable, of course, but now I'd succeeded in digging such a deep hole for myself that I fully expected to emerge from a pile of fresh, red soil in Sydney, blinking in the sunlight like a bewildered mole. I now had just two months to completely rewrite my novel. Perfectly do-able, if I didn't sleep at all during that time, or succumb to a real dose of writer's block or depression, a scenario that was now eminently possible.

Paul popped his head around the door again.

'Sorry to interrupt, Adam, but come and look at this.'

I followed him, zombie-like into the hallway, where he'd been fitting the hall radiator. He warned me to be careful, as several of the floorboards had been taken up and he didn't want me having a nasty accident.

'Look, we found something,' he said, proffering a cobwebbed and dusty old hessian shopping bag.

'Where was this then?' I asked.

'Down there, under a loose floorboard,' he replied.

I took the bag from him and looked inside. There was a block of some two hundred or more yellowing sheets of paper, A4 in size; perhaps a little larger - maybe it was the old foolscap size that my dad always used to refer to – all neatly tied together with string. I examined it more closely, and realized that it was a manuscript, entitled 'Mary Falls in Love' by Thomas M. Bingham. I put two and two together and was pretty sure I'd got four for a change. Surely, this was what Bingham had sent to Alison for safe keeping; one of the items he'd referred to in the very letter that Edgecliffe's had just sent me. Hidden under the hallway floorboards of all places! She'd put it somewhere safe alright, though I'm sure old Thomas would have been happy with the bedside locker. I'm no Sherlock Holmes, but it looked to me as if she'd simply forgotten all about the hidden manuscript, after her brother had died at the hands of the Gestapo. I thanked Paul for finding it and left him and Pete to their work. I went back to the living room and carefully removed the string. My first impression was that the title of the book was not what I was expecting. I'd got it into my head that this man wrote gritty, realistic stuff in the style of, say, Steinbeck for example, and this soppy title, 'Mary Falls in Love' sounded more like a Mills and Boone-style romance novel for the weaker-headed, drippier members of the opposite sex. Maybe it was meant to be ironic, I don't know. I turned the page. It was all written in pencil. This made sense, and confirmed my suspicions that it had been written while inside the camp. The Germans would hardly have supplied him with a nice new Royal typewriter, even if they were aware of who he was. I read the first two pages, which, sadly, were truly awful. It was turgid stuff. Utter bilge, I have to say. I struggled through ten more. Just harmless, light, non-descript, of its time, fluffy romantic rubbish. I was expecting something that reflected the hardships that he and his friends were undoubtedly facing on a daily basis, not this tosh. Whether he was deliberately blotting out all the unpleasantness of the concentration camp and was writing something soppy just for his sister to read, or if he'd decided to have a stab at the Woman's magazine serial market, I couldn't say, but somehow I just couldn't see it improving as it progressed. I suddenly felt very frustrated. I really wished I could have read more about this man on the internet, but, of course, I hadn't got a computer any more. I decided that the time was right to go and buy another laptop, as the odds of having my own returned had now sunk to around a million to one.

Deeply disappointed after my initial excitement, I laid the old manuscript to one side, grabbed my coat and my overworked, underpaid little credit card, and set off for Megan-Byte, the computer shop, conveniently situated a few hundred yards past the end of my road. Megan, the eponymous owner, was making a house call on her bicycle to tend to a PC that had a nasty virus; the modern equivalent of a 1950s district nurse or midwife visiting a sick patient at home I suppose. Her husband and business partner, Ron, a large, amiable bald-headed fellow, was looking after the shop until she returned. I explained to him that I needed a new laptop and didn't want to spend over

£400. Actually, I didn't want to spend anything at all; a bit like that Irish thug at Birmingham International, but I drew the line at coshing Ron senseless and nicking off with one. Regardless of our many failings and frailties, we Eve's are honest folk. Ron selected a few machines and placed them on the counter. He then set about comparing their memories, functions and so on, and I, naturally, glazed over instantly, like a very shallow saucerful of water in a deep-freeze.

'This one has a Pentangle Radioactive Food Processor with seventeen million Ryan Giggs of memory,' he said - or at least it sounded a bit like that - and I tried to look impressed, even though I didn't have the faintest idea what he was on about. I was reminded of those car ads on TV, where they seem to make a big deal of the fact that the vehicle has a ZETEC engine. I'm sure these ad agencies just invent silly hi-tech-sounding names such as that, and bandy them around until we're all brainwashed into believing that having a ZETEC engine is an absolute prerequisite if one is looking forward to a lifetime of happy, stress-free motoring. The fact that no one on this earth has a clue what one is or what it does is neither here nor there. We just fall for the bullshit time after time. The same applies to all those creams and potions that women feel the need to buy in order to combat the seven signs of ageing - whatever they are. If there was a liposome and a few theramides in it, my ex-wife wanted it, and couldn't wait to get it home so that she could smear it all over her body and watch it do precisely nothing.

Ron, bless him, could see that I clearly didn't have a clue, so he leaned over the cluttered counter and whispered conspiratorially, 'I'd buy this one. It's £385 and it's a laptop.'

I told him to throw in a few free lipozomes and a ZETEC and I'd take it.

When I got back, Paul and Pete were having their lunch in the van, and they warned me to watch where I was walking when I got inside. Getting from the front doorway to my living room was not dissimilar to walking the plank. I never realized what havoc a few radiators would cause. Honestly, I thought I'd never be straight again! I unpacked the laptop and tried to make sense of the instructions. Luckily, they were written in such a way that a ten-year-old boy could understand them. I say luckily, because I happen to have a ten-year-old boy. I made a mental note to ring him after school and con him into setting the thing up for me, in return for a new PlayStation game. I turned my attention once more to Thomas Bingham. After falling at the first hurdle with my new computer, partly due to being an awful technophobe, and partly because of my selective dyslexia (I seem to be able to read anything but an instruction manual) I picked up the old manuscript again. I absent-mindedly riffled through the pages, and forgive me for digressing here, but if this memoir ever sees the light of day in published form, could I just mention to whomever is proof-reading this that I meant riffled, nor rifled, so please refrain from 'correcting' it. Riffling is what magician's do with cards and rifled is something else altogether. Thank you!

So I riffled through it to see how much writing there was, and stopped randomly near the middle. I glanced down at the text and read a few lines to see if it had miraculously improved, and it was immediately obvious that what I was reading was not of the same ilk as the nondescript waffle that preceded it. I flicked (or riffled) back several pages, and suddenly came across another title page. It read, 'The

Grave Digger' by Thomas M. Bingham. At first, I could make no sense of this at all. The first novel just ended, unfinished, and this one took over. I turned to the back, and spotted that 'The Grave Digger' text ended, and the soppy romance story commenced again for the final ten or so pages. What on earth could it mean? There was no logical explanation, unless...

Unless, parcels sent home were scrutinized by the guards. Why, of course! That was it. Prisoners were very occasionally allowed to receive letters and send them too, but just as our modern English prisons check for hidden messages in correspondence, files in cakes, cannabis in cigarettes and what have you, so must the wartime post have been similarly examined. Bingham had hinted in his letter that there was a German guard who was nicer than some. Maybe the writer thought that anyone looking at his novel would scan the first section and deem it to be harmless. He had presumably gambled that anyone searching for propaganda or secret messages would have given up and lost the will to live after suffering the first twenty pages of 'Mary falls in Love', and let it pass. If this was what actually happened, and it was obviously just speculation on my part, Bingham had played a dangerous game and got away with it. From what I'd heard about him so far, he was not averse to living dangerously.

I made yet another pot of tea and turned the pages until I found 'The Grave Digger'. I needed something to distract me from my woes, as my recent conversation with Rob Wakefield had left my nerves jangling. I figured that this would calm me down a bit, but in truth, I also had another motive. If the story was good, then Edgecliffe's would surely be interested in publishing it. It would be like discovering a new Steinbeck that had been lost in an attic.

The 1940s were a long time ago, but famous writers of that period still had legions of loyal fans, I presumed. This old wad of yellowing paper could potentially make me a lot of money. Or could it? I wasn't sure of the law where this kind of thing was concerned. If, for example, Bingham still had living relatives, wouldn't they be entitled to every penny, and not me? I thought about this for a few moments, and came to the decision that it didn't matter. If someone decided to toss me a few quid for my trouble, all well and good. If not, I'd be a bit miffed, certainly, but it was my duty to hand this over to Edgecliffe's regardless. I just hoped, for everyone's sake, that 'The Grave Digger' turned out to be a lot better than 'Mary falls in Love'. If not, no one would touch it with a barge pole.

I checked that the plumbers were happy and gainfully employed, which they were, closed the living room door to deaden the sound of their banging and clattering, put my feet up on the coffee table and began to read.

I was still reading at midnight, albeit with one eye, and I was reduced to applying liberal coatings of saliva to that in order to keep it going. I simply could not put the book down; it was so riveting. It told a story of concentration camp life that was in parts harrowing, poignant, farcical, tragic and even humorous. It was 'Schindler's List', 'The Great Escape' and 'The Diary of Anne Frank' all rolled into one, with a host of believable characters and a nail-biter of a plot. The best thing I had read in a long time, and it was a testament to how good the book was that I persevered in spite of the shaky, often hard-to-decipher handwriting, the crossings out and the many corrections. Reading a book of real quality and gravitas such as this also served to put me in my place. Writing my kind of light, flippant, lazy, scantily- researched novel was a piece of cake compared to this. Each harrowing, emotional chapter must have been agonizing for him to get down on paper. Each sentence must have left him drained and tearful. What made it all the more poignant was that this was real life and death that he was living through and writing about, and not just the product of a vivid imagination, typed in the cosy study of some London mansion or other, with a roaring fire in the hearth, a Labrador at his feet and a gin and tonic at his side.

I glanced at the clock. I had five pages to read and only then would I go to bed. I slipped out to the kitchen and washed my face in cold water, which seemed to do the trick, at least temporarily. I devoured the next few pages, desperate to find out how this could possibly end, and then it did. Abruptly. In fact, it ended halfway through a sentence.

Frustrated isn't a big enough word to describe how I felt at that juncture. It was as if Halle Berry had slipped naked into my bed, tenderly kissed me and whispered, 'Make love to me, Adam,' and then disappeared in a puff of smoke. I flicked feverishly through the manuscript to see if pages had been displaced, and the gripping finale was hiding amongst the cloyingly sentimental pages of 'Mary Falls in Love'. It wasn't. I had been robbed of my literary orgasm. I was bereft.

Not only had I not been granted my climax after hours and hours of literary foreplay, I now also had nothing to offer to Edgecliffe's. I couldn't imagine them being eager to publish a novel that lacked an ending, and neither could I see them employing a ghost writer to finish it off. That would have been unethical. It would have been tantamount to cheating, and a company like Edgecliffe's might well not stoop that low. They were far too old-school for that. There was only one alternative. I would have to finish it myself.

Chapter 10

I opened the front door in my dressing gown. I'll just pause for a second so that you can now say, 'I didn't know there was a front door in your dressing gown!' Really, I am disappointed in you, I have to say. That joke is around fifty years old, if it's a day.

I had overslept, due to my late night reading session, and I'd forgotten that Katie was dropping my son, James, around to set up my new computer. James, dressed in his cricket whites and carrying a bat and ball, dispensed with tedious formalities such as 'hello dad' and instead informed me that he was going into the garden, adding that I was bowling and he was batting.

Katie looked lovely in a skimpy top and tight jeans, in sharp contrast to her ex, who was modelling a sweaty vest, boxer shorts with gaping hole at the front, and the aforementioned shabby tartan dressing gown. My hair looked as if someone had tried to comb it with a garden rake, and two days-worth of stubble was sprouting through my chin. To my credit though, I was nibbling on an apple, which at least gave the impression that my body was a temple, albeit a ruined one. I asked her how she was and meant it.

'Oh, you know, not great really,' she replied, looking down at the ground.

'How's Mark?' I asked. This time I couldn't care less.

'Change the subject,' she frowned. 'Lauren says hello. She was going to pop in herself, but she's gone out with her mates instead. You know what they're like at that age.'

'No problem,' I lied. 'Fancy coming in for a cup of tea? We can sit in the garden. It just about holds three people if I move the big plant pot.'

Katie ran her hand through her hair, something she often did that always made me want to have sex with her, there and then. She seemed distracted. 'I'd better not. I told him I'd be back.'

'Ah, come on, what's the harm for five minutes?' I pleaded.

'Stop tempting me.'

'I'm Adam,' I replied. 'Tempting you into gardens is what I do. Want a bite of my apple?'

'I don't!' she smiled. 'Anyway, I thought that was Eve who did that. You'll be trying to show me your snake next.'

'More of a slow worm nowadays. And a redundant one at that.'

Katie smiled a sad smile that turned my stomach inside out.

'Listen, I have to get back,' she said. 'He likes his lunch on the table when he walks through the door. I'll stay for a drink next time.'

'Hope so,' I said. 'I'll go and play cricket with James for a bit then. Otherwise he might refuse to set up my new laptop for me.'

'See you soon, Adam,' Katie said, turning to go.

'Bye!' I sighed. I called after her as she walked to the gate. 'I never demanded my dinner when I got home from work, did I?'

Katie unlocked her car and got in. She wound down the window. 'That's only because you never went anywhere to work! Bye Adam.'

And with that, she was gone.

I wandered through to my postage stamp of a garden to do my fatherly duty, and tried not to bowl James out too often, otherwise he had a tendency to sulk. After around an hour, when we'd lost all four tennis balls over Barbara's garden, we went inside and set about the new laptop, or at least, James did. I sat in the kitchen nursing a mug of tea, and thinking deep thoughts about what I'd had and lost.

*

For someone with two broken wrists, depression, writer's block, a lost-forever novel and a recently discovered novel, both with their final chapters missing, I was doing rather well, I thought. For a start, I had a lovely new central heating system that came on when it was asked to, or even of its own accord when the time was right, or the indoor temperature had dropped below 19 degrees. I also had a new, efficient laptop, thanks to my ten-year-old son, James, so I was able to Google things again, and the first thing I Googled was, 'Who lost his manuscript on a train'. I admit I was rather disappointed when Google didn't say that it was me. Still, we can't expect it to know everything I suppose, but it did know all about Ernest Hemingway, who lost virtually everything he'd ever typed in one fell swoop, when he left his suitcase on the train, and was never to see it again. This, however, was apparently the making of him. Champing at the bit to recreate his original ideas, he wrote everything again, in a new, stripped down, less fussy style which was no doubt the result of his eagerness to get it onto paper before he completely forgot it all. Ironically, it was this new style that was the reason for his success. Good stories simply and economically told, in a nutshell. I must say, this little bit of Googling had been the fillip that I needed. If Hemingway could start from scratch and become even better than he used to be, then so could I. I would rise, Pat Phoenix-like from the ashes of The Copy Shop and write the whole bloody novel again, but this time, sparser, stripped down and Hemingway-like. If Rob Wakefield rang, I would look him square on and tell him the truth, the whole truth and nothing like the truth, so help me Rob. My book was lost forever, but if he would give me three or four months, and not my original two, I would hand him his bestseller on a plate with lettuce around it, and we would both end up better off.

But before I felt up to tackling that, I decided to complete Thomas Bingham's masterpiece. I figured that, if I could crack that, my own book would be a doddle afterwards. My first problem was continuity. Thomas had written everything in his own hand, which was causing me a big headache. I couldn't write the last chapter on my new laptop and present Edgecliffe's with a print-out, for obvious reasons, and I also couldn't write it on my five quid vintage Corona typewriter that I'd bought from a bric-a-brac sale for decorative purposes. The period was about right, but why would the Germans have suddenly allowed Bingham a typewriter to write a tale about the cruelty and hardship of a concentration camp, or even a sloppy romance novel, come to that? I eventually decided to write the chapter using my laptop for the time being, while I pondered the conundrum of presentation. This cosmetic problem was nothing, however, compared to the nightmare of actually writing the last chapter. For a start, I had no idea how Bingham had intended to end this story, though several possible endings did immediately present themselves. Did I go for heartbreak and devastation, bittersweet, hopeful, happy, the cliff hanger, what?

Then there was the issue of style. The way we write is like a fingerprint; it's individual and unique. Could I mimic his style and get away with it for just one concluding chapter? There was only one way to find out, and that was to knuckle down to it, write and rewrite until I found his voice; until I tapped into his mind and hijacked his identity. However, before I did that, I wanted to watch Crimewatch U.K. on the telly. I set the video recorder so that I could watch it several times, and lay across the settee, excited, with a bag of peanuts and a cup of Shiraz for company.

Seeing it all unfold was very spooky indeed. I saw Jeremy, or at least an actor who bore a passing resemblance to him, treading the familiar path from train platform to car park, carrying my laptop bag, or at least an actor bag that bore a passing resemblance to it. I saw him place the bag on his car roof while he searched for his keys, and I found myself begging him to look behind him, like kids do at the pantomime. Then, looming out of the darkness, the stocky, shaven-headed Irishman snarling, 'Give me yer fekking laptop there nye!' followed by loads of fake violence and wobbly camera work. Cue presenter, looking grave and telling us that this monster needed to be caught before he did it again.

As soon as the item had finished, I rang Jeremy out of politeness, and asked if he was okay. His sigh spoke volumes so I left it at that. It must have been interesting, watching himself get beaten up on primetime television. I told him I'd watched the programme and added that I thought the actor was marginally better looking than he was. It was just my way of cheering him up, and he took it like a man. As soon as I had replaced the receiver, the phone rang again. I had an over-excited Barbara from next door on the line now, telling me she'd just seen my laptop on Crimewatch. I took advantage of the fact that she was paying for the call and asked her if she knew of a Miss Alison Bingham, and once the fog of old age had cleared, she said yes, of course, it was the woman who sold her house to Mr Jennings the teacher who sold it to Mr Lewis the fireman who sold it to me. She'd never known the lady, but Barbara was vaguely aware that Alison Bingham had a famous brother who was killed in the war. Mr Jennings, who lived in my house after Alison but before Mr Lewis (are you following this?) reckoned she – Alison Bingham I'm referring to - was a nice lady, if a bit eccentric. Apparently, continued Barbara, she was prone to mislaying stuff on a regular basis and got battier with each coming year. Mr Jennings once told Barbara that the woman had left a loaf of brown bread on his car roof, and he'd driven off with it still there. Remarkably, it had only fallen off onto his bonnet when he reached Dudley, where his aunt lived, so he'd handed it to the aunt as a gift and they'd made toast with it. This was all very interesting, and tallied perfectly with the 'forgotten manuscript under the floorboards' discovery. It's rather wonderful when all the strands come together, don't you think?

I was about to try and bring the conversation to a halt when I remembered something.

'Barbara,' I asked, 'did you say your Henry was a sales rep, before he retired?'

'Yes,' she replied. 'For an office stationery company in Birmingham called Holyhead's, why?'

'Oh, just a long shot really. I know you keep a lot of his old stuff in your garage, you hoarder you! I don't suppose for one minute you still have any reams of paper in there do you? I need some of that old-style foolscap-sized stuff for a job I'm working on and they probably don't make it nowadays.'

'It's easier to tell you what *isn't* in my garage,' laughed Barbara. 'I'll have a look in the morning for you if you like. It would probably be yellow with age now and damp, even if there was any. I don't think that would be much good to you.'

'You'd be surprised,' I replied. 'I like my paper like I like my women. Yellow and damp.'

I put the phone down and gave myself a quizzical look in the living room mirror. I did not have the faintest notion what that last comment of mine was supposed to mean.

That evening, and for the rest of that week, I locked myself away in my room, writing and rewriting that last chapter. To begin with, my efforts were laughable, which is the desired effect when one writes comedy, my usual vehicle, but when one is delving into man's inhumanity to man and all that kind of thing, 'laughable' is not

93

particularly what one strives for. However, long and tortuous though the journey undoubtedly was, I did eventually begin to see a glimmer of light at the end of the tunnel, and inch by inch I got under the skin of this great writer and, *I* think anyway, pulled it off in grand style. In fact, I was rather chuffed, not to mention surprised at myself. I'd delivered a rather dramatic, uplifting conclusion to Thomas Bingham's wonderful masterpiece, and after rereading it around fifty times, altering a word here, a comma there, I felt justifiably proud of it. The plot flowed; there was no discernable change in the writing style, nothing that pointed to a ghost-written conclusion. My ending would have them weeping in the aisles, I was convinced of it.

Barbara, true to her word, rummaged around in her garage and came up trumps. She had discovered a cardboard boxful of foolscap, or imperial, or whatever the hell it was called, and it was pretty much the same as Bingham had used. Cheap, wartime utility writing paper, coarse, nasty and yellowing. Perfect, in other words! I experimented with several grades and makes of pencil until I found one identical to the sort he had used. Now came the real challenge. Luckily, Bingham's handwriting was not *too* dissimilar to mine, but it was smaller, more angled to the right and had that copperplate neatness that was drummed into every young child back then, before illiterate scrawl became *de rigueur*. He constructed his 'Y's very differently to mine though, and also his 'G's and 'B's, so I would have to concentrate. I took a sheet of Barbara's paper and copied a page of his manuscript. I had got into his head as a writer. Now I had to get into his head as a writer, if you'll excuse the clever wordplay. If anything, this was going to prove even more difficult than creating his last chapter. There had to be a seamless join or I'd be sussed. Even Blind Pew could have spotted that my first attempt was a blatant forgery, let alone a sharp-eyed publisher. There was obviously still a lot of work to be done.

I practised his handwriting style over and over until it gradually started to feel more natural to me, and when I was happy, I knocked it on the head for the day. The next morning after breakfast, I set about copying out the final chapter that I'd written. After a few false starts, I found my rhythm and was motoring along, but the concentration it required was such that I had to take a break every now and again to compose myself. During one such break, I popped upstairs to take a shower, and while doing so, it dawned on me that I had been going about things the wrong way. I towelled myself dry, slipped on my boxer shorts and returned to my writing room, impatient to try something out. I'd realized that it would be far easier for me if I quickly printed out the text from my laptop, so that I could place it directly next to my hand-written sheet, rather than having to keep staring at the laptop screen and scrolling down all the time. I looked in the cupboard where I keep my printer paper, and to my dismay, all I found was the empty packet. This meant another trip to Megan-Byte, which I could have done without. What I did find, however, was a bright orange nylon Tina Turner wig, and before you jump to the conclusion that I am weird (I am as it happens, but not in that way) can I just explain to you what it was doing in my stationery cupboard? I presume your answer will be in the affirmative, so I will proceed. My daughter, Lauren, bought the thing a few years back for a fancy dress party, at the time when I was still with my wife, Katie, and afterwards, she decided to dress my son up as Tina Turner – he was all of five at the time and still did what his big sister told him to do, no matter how stupid the request. She put make-up on his little chubby face (not sure how I felt about that), added the nylon wig, a pink 'My Little Pony' vest, a small skirt and a pair of her tall, shiny black boots, which looked more like waders on him. By now, we were all pretty much in hysterics, I have to say. Then, to round it off, she handed him an empty toilet roll tube, his makeshift microphone, and encouraged him to put on a show for his parents. After a brief rehearsal period in the front room, he tottered into the living room again, followed by Lauren who seemed to be having a fit; she was laughing so much, and little James starting shouting, 'Nutbush City Limits, Grrr! Grrr! Nutbush City Limits Grrr! Grr!' Through his toilet roll. I honestly thought I would wet myself, it was so funny. The thing that really cracked me up, though, was the mysterious 'Grrr Grrr!' bit, which I don't remember being in the original version. Perhaps it was an attempt at a raunchy guitar sound, I don't know. I can only speculate. It became even funnier when he became indignant that we were not taking his show seriously, and he started yelling 'Shurrup! Shurrup!' through his toilet roll at us and petulantly stamping his foot.

I grabbed the wig, put it on and took a look at myself in the living room mirror. Jeez! It was grotesque, but it set off another fit of uncontrollable laughter. I make no apology for the fact that we Eve's are notorious gigglers. Me, my brother Steve, our mother, we're all as bad. When we get started, it's easier to stop a two-hundred miles-an-hour diesel train. Just when we think we've got it out of our systems, it starts again, only worse, if anything. It was still engulfing me in uncontrollable waves when I heard a strange scratching sound that seemed to be coming from the back door - the one that leads to the garden and the entry between my house and my neighbours on the left side. I went to investigate, and found Widdle the cat on its hind legs, scratching away at the glass and demanding to be let in. I opened the door and bent down to say hello, and it leapt into my arms. Obviously, that tin of tuna chunks had created a bond between us every bit as strong as the one shared by Androcles and his lion. Little Widdle had come back for more of the same, by the looks of it. Wasn't that woman down the road feeding the little thing? And was that perhaps why Puddles had decided to sling his hook, I wondered.

I was about to repair to the kitchen to see if I had another tin stashed away, when Widdle demonstrated to me why she had been christened thus. She suddenly peed right down my freshly-bathed chest and all over my clean-on boxers.

'You little bugger!' I growled, somewhat miffed, adding with mock severity, 'I am now going to kill you, and may the Lord have mercy on all nine of your souls.'

It was at this precise juncture that I heard a voice calling my name. I turned around, and saw a police officer the size of a substantial brick lavatory, blotting out my light again like a total eclipse of the sun in a helmet.

'Put the cat down, Mr Eve,' he demanded sternly. So I did. I was rather hoping that the ground would open up and swallow me right there and then, because I had just realized how I must have looked. Even worse, any form of logical explanation would have been so difficult to pull off that I found myself unable to even attempt one. I just stood there looking and feeling as if I'd suffered a stroke, with my mouth open, and my eyes staring in an unfocussed kind of way.

'Mr Eve, can I ask why you are almost naked and dressed up as David Bowie?' asked the officer, stepping into the house without asking.

'I'm not dressed up as David Bowie,' I replied, somewhat indignantly. 'It's Tina Turner.'

I realized as soon as the words had left my mouth that this hadn't done me any favours.

'I've just had a shower; I found it in that cupboard – the wig I mean, not the shower, that's upstairs – and I just tried it on for a laugh.'

'I see,' said the policeman, though he quite plainly didn't. 'Putting that aside for one moment, what did I just hear you say to the cat?'

'Erm, about the tin of tuna, do you mean?'

'Mr Eve, we both know you never mentioned a tin of tuna. You said something along the lines of, you little bastard, I am going to kill you, and may the Lord have mercy upon your soul.'

I took issue with his substitution of 'bastard' for 'bugger', but I let it pass.

'I was being flippant,' I said, removing the wig and slinging it onto the coffee table in a fit of pique. 'Old Widdle had just peed all down me. You don't think I'd really kill a cat for something silly like that do you?'

'So what would you kill a cat for, Mr Eve?'

'Well nothing, of course,' I assured him, exasperated and a bit tired of his moronic interrogation technique. 'I'm a bloody animal lover. Everybody knows that round here. Ask them! My dog, Len, has not long died and I've been heartbroken. I had him for fourteen years. I was even thinking of adopting one of those drug mules from a donkey sanctuary recently, till my mate Darrell told me I'd got the wrong end of the stick.'

The policeman kept staring at me with a particularly beady eye, which was very disconcerting. He asked me to sit down, sat opposite me and removed his helmet.

'Did you kill your dog, Len, as well? Did he maybe annoy you by digging up your garden, looking for bones? Is this what sets you off?'

I'd more than had enough of this bloke now, and I told him so.

'What, if anything, are you bloody on about?' I snapped.

The policeman stood up, and for a horrible second, I thought I was about to become the victim of police brutality.

'Will you please get dressed, shut the cat in the living room and accompany me outside,' he barked. I did what I was told. He proceeded in an easterly direction through my front door and made his way towards the front gate. I followed him into the street and he paused at the three black bin bags that were propped up against my garden wall, awaiting collection.

'I take it that these are yours?' he asked. I replied in the affirmative. 'Please open them up for me.'

Now he was taking me into new and uncharted territory. I gave him a quizzical look and untied the knot on bag number one. He looked inside.

'Open the next one, if you would,' he snapped. I opened it up. Strangely, it too was full of evil-smelling garbage.

'Now the third one,' he said.

I opened the bag, and immediately recoiled in horror at what I saw. Staring up at me was the face of a dead cat. Beneath it, there appeared to be more cats in varying degrees of decomposition. Three, four, five, maybe more. It was hard to say. Flies were buzzing loudly inside the evil-smelling bag. I turned away in disgust.

'Adam Eve,' said the policeman sadly, 'I am arresting...'

'Now hang on a minute!' I interrupted. 'This is nothing to do with me whatsoever. This isn't my bin bag. I remember now, I only put two out. Someone else has put this here to incriminate me. I love animals. I would never do anything as evil as this, you have to believe me.'

My mind was racing. I felt sick. The Curtain Twitcher was observing us over the road, I could see her gawping from her bay window. An article in the free paper, next to the one about The Copy Shop burning down, suddenly came into my head. All over town, people were losing their cats. Of course! It wasn't just the lady down the road, it was an epidemic. I'd seen a piece about it. The headline was, let me think, let me think...The Purr-muda Triangle. And this imbecile thinks it's me!

'Who told you about these cats?' I demanded. 'Tell me who put you onto this?'

'So you do admit to killing them, Mr Eve?' he said.

'No, I fucking well do not!' I yelled back at him. 'Now can we go back into my house and sort this out, or would you prefer to humiliate me in front of my neighbours, even though I've done nothing?'

'Neither,' he replied. 'You will have to come with me to the station I'm afraid, and give a statement. Adam Eve, you are under arrest. You don't have to say anything...'

'Oh don't worry,' I said, shaking now, 'I'm going to say something alright.'

Chapter 11

Having previously never even dropped a piece of litter, I was now a mass moggie murderer, apparently. Being arrested was downright embarrassing. I was allowed one phone call and then left in a cell for the best part of an hour, scared stiff. After careful consideration, I decided against going fifty-fifty and asking the audience, and instead phoned a friend, Mr Edward Chance the solicitor, of Norfolk & Chance - yes, really, you couldn't make it up – who, when he arrived an hour later, assured the dim-witted rozzers that I was somewhat purer than driven snow, and made Mother Teresa look like an evil drug trafficker by comparison. After they had listened carefully to his impassioned defence, they duly informed me that I was being charged with cruelty to animals. Then there was a lot of back and forth argy-bargy between Mr Chance and the policemen which culminated in my being '47-3 police bailed' (whatever that meant) and allowed to go home, as long as I promised not to leave the country, wipe out any more of the fast-dwindling local pet population on a whim, or dance naked in the high street wearing a Tina Turner wig. I had repeatedly demanded to know who had stitched me up, but was met with a blank refusal to divulge their information.

I spent a sleepless night, tossing and turning, desperately trying to fathom out what had happened to me, and why. I hadn't killed any cats and dumped them in a bin bag, in case you're wondering, so obviously someone else had and chosen my house to offload the sorry little corpses. Was I randomly chosen? I would have guessed yes, had not the culprit also elected to anonymously tip off the police. Surely, if a twisted psycho with a sack full of murdered cats slung over his back had passed my house and decided that here was the perfect spot to offload them, he would simply have done the evil deed and walked swiftly on into the night. I just couldn't see him bothering to finger me unless he held a grudge, could you? Someone had phoned the police and presumably told them that they had seen me dropping the bag there. The more I thought about this, the less sense it made. If I had merely dropped a black bag by my wall, how could they know that it was full of dead cats? Did they wait for me to go back inside and then say to themselves, 'I wonder if there are dead cats in that one. I'll just take a peek'? After all, I'm hardly likely to bring piles of dead cats out of my front door in a wheel barrow and shovel them into the bag in the street, am I?

It was then that I had an idea, but it would have to wait until morning. In the meantime, I tried to take my mind of things by thinking of Halle Berry striding out of the sea in that James Bond film. I have to report that it stopped the turning but not the tossing. Still, one out of two ain't bad.

I skipped breakfast and walked over the road, to the house immediately to the left of old Curtain Twitcher. I reckoned that she was loving all this. A few years back, when she lived at her previous bungalow a few streets away, I'd been taking Len, my faithful dog, for his evening constitutional, when he'd crouched down, ready to do his stuff, right outside her house. Well, when you have to go, you have to go, and I'm not one of those idiot pet owners without poop scoopers who try to drag them away as they're doing it. All you end up with then is a line of little mini-turds spanning ten yards or more, which is even worse than one big nasty pile. I stood around whistling a jaunty tune, scooper and old Tesco bag in my pocket, at the ready, but on this occasion, no business resulted. I think it was the whole packet of salted nuts that he'd nicked out of my shopping bag the previous day that was to blame. They must have given him constipation. All the time this was happening, this woman was staring at us through the nets, ready to pounce. As we walked away, she shot out of her front door and screamed, banshee-like, 'Are you going to pick that up?' I looked around me theatrically, and replied, 'Pick what up, exactly?' whereupon she charged down the path and began to examine the pavement, before sheepishly returning to her bungalow, a spent force. To compound her misery, I later caught her chucking a crisp packet out of her car window, which I helpfully dropped back into her car with a 'tut tut'.

Since then, relations have been frosty, and to make matters worse, the silly old cow decided to buy a house directly opposite me, by sheer chance, I hasten to add. I doubt if she'd have done so on purpose. You should have seen her face when I greeted her one morning as she picked up her milk bottles in her ghastly pink nylon dressing gown.

Thankfully, I was not visiting her on this occasion (or any other if I could help it), but her long-suffering next-door neighbour, Darrell, who is a carpenter. Darrell was the man who fitted my new windows and hung a couple of doors for me, when I first bought the house. He was around fifty-five, but looked younger, and he was possibly the world's most boring teller of stories, if you can call an incoherent ramble that doesn't go anywhere a story. When he was around my house for days on end, working on my windows, I would dread him stopping work to drink the tea I had made for him (which, incidentally, he took with four sugars) because I knew that it was only a matter of seconds before a Darrell anecdote would follow. These came with no warning and from nowhere. They sometimes lasted for hours, and omitted no detail, however minute, inconsequential or irrelevant to the thrust of the plot, ending just as abruptly as they began, with me none the wiser. Nor would they begin as a consequence of or a response to something I had just said. They were not apropos of anything at all. Darrell would pick up his sickly sweet, tooth-dissolving beverage and just launch into it, usually beginning with the expression that I came to dread, 'No, only...'

As in, 'No, only, I was going out the other Wednesday. Tell a lie, it was Tuesday - I know that because Jim, my brother, was in The Nag's Head, and he only goes there on Tuesdays. Any road, I saw Barry the electrician – you know him - fat chap, supports the Albion - and he said that Arthur, the local copper, had arrested two chaps from Willenhall, tell a lie, Wednesbury, no, it was Willenhall - I was right - for stealing a bike that belonged to Gordon who works down the Labour Club, him who lost his wife, Doris, was it? Apologies, Doreen, I knew it would come to me. She was the one that had the twins. One was black, remember? Any road...'

And so it would go on, meandering into cul-de-sacs, backtracking, getting lost and going nowhere slowly, until suddenly, Darrell would conclude with something along the lines of, '...and Bill was still playing darts.' and suddenly it would all be over. There was no beginning, middle or end, and no plot. There was no punch line, no point, nothing. He was merely relating a slice of his life as it happened, and when the coin meter ran out in what passed for his brain, he stopped, and began sawing and sanding again.

I rapped on his front door and hoped against hope that this wasn't one of his meandering anecdote days. With all the stress I was going through, I didn't think I could stand it. Darrell opened the door and grinned at me. He flicked the nub end of his withered little roll-up onto the grass and invited me in. He was wearing denim dungarees and his hair was coated with yellow sawdust.

'Just finishing Mavis's conservatory windows,' he said as I followed him through to his large shed in the garden, 'no, only, I've got to pop to Brum this afternoon, well, I say afternoon, but...'

'Sorry to interrupt, Daz,' I said somewhat abruptly, 'but this is pretty urgent, mate. I need your help. Remember when you had a break-in and the ratbags stole all your tools?'

'I think I'd remember that, ar!'

'And you installed CCTV afterwards didn't you?'

'Ar, they nearly bankrupted me, the little bastards. I had to buy pretty much everythin' again.'

'Did you install it at the front of the house or just the back, where your workshop is?'

'Both,' said Darrell, 'just in case they tried to take me van. I parks me van at the front, and me tools am at the back in the workshop.'

'Was your CCTV on last night, by any chance? The one at the front I mean. I daresay it would show my house wouldn't it?' I looked down and realized that both my hands were curled up tightly into fists. I relaxed them. It happens while I'm having my teeth drilled as well.

'Ar, you can see some of your house in it. Why, wassup?'

'Can I make you and me a cup of tea, while I take a look at the footage?' I asked. 'If you're busy, just carry on. I need to study that film. It's very, very important.'

'Course,' smiled Darrell. 'There's the kitchen. Teabags in that jar, milk in the fridge, mugs in that cupboard. Oh, and I only take three and a half now. I'm cutting down. Sugar's over there, in that bucket. I'll wind back last night's show and leave you to it!'

I made the tea and began to smirk at the memory of a practical joke that my ex-wife, Katie, had played on him while he was at our family home, fitting skirting boards, seven or so years back. She had stirred twelve heaped sugars into his tea and handed it to him with a straight face as he worked. She retrieved the empty cup half an hour later, and the sweet-toothed carpenter never uttered a word.

Darrell set up the equipment for me, pressed the start button and left me to it. God, it was monotonous viewing. It was the video equivalent of one of Darrell's monologues, come to think of it. All I could see was the edge of his white van and the top section of my wall. I could just about make out my two bin bags, but there was no sign of the third. Not yet. Occasionally, people walked by, but no one was lingering. I pressed 'fast forward', and now the people shot past as if they were competing in an Olympic walking race. Cars whipped back and forth at a thousand miles per hour, but still no one with a black bin bag. Then, just as I was about to take a rest and rub my tired eyes, I saw it. I stopped the film, pressed rewind and stopped it again. I bit my nails to the quick and pressed play. It may well have been the world's most boring film prior to this, but now it was suddenly a mesmerising thriller. A figure, blurred and close up in the lens, was crossing the road furtively, lugging a bin bag in its wake. She – it was a she! – looked around furtively and dumped it next to mine, before briskly striding back across the road for her close-up. Oh, my prophetic soul! It was none other than Curtain Twitcher. I rewound and watched it again, my blood boiling now. I watched a third time and pressed 'stop'. I'd seen enough. I ran out to Darrell's shed and knocked on his door. He emerged coughing and spluttering from all the sawdust he'd been ingesting and asked if it had been of any use, and I replied in the affirmative, with knobs on, to the power of ten, and then some. I explained that the police were involved and they'd need to see his film. I didn't wish to name names at this stage, but I did rather indiscreetly mention that it was all about catching the Stourbridge Cat Killer, which interested him more than somewhat. It turns out that Darrell's beloved moggie, Wilf Jenkins, had gone missing just after Curtain Twitcher moved in next door. She'd helped him look for it, in fact. I bit my lip and thanked him for his time, promising to drop the tape back as soon as the police had examined it.

I shot over the road, back to my house, and immediately dialled the officer who had arrested me. He was out on the beat, I was told, no doubt making other innocent people's lives a complete misery, but the desk sergeant promised that he'd get him to ring me as soon as he was able. I took advantage of the lull to ring Graham Bateman at

Edgecliffe's. His secretary insisted that he was too busy to take my call, but I dug my heels in and said it was extremely important.

'May I ask what it's concerning?' she asked.

'Yes,' I replied.

There was a strained silence.

'Erm, what's it concerning?' she asked.

'I'm not telling you,' I replied.

'But, you said...'

'I said you could ask. I didn't say I'd tell you.'

There was another strained silence. Then Mr Bateman answered. He sounded a bit impatient.

I told him who I was, and he asked if I'd enjoyed the book. I explained that, as yet, it had not arrived, and he promised to skin his secretary alive upon replacing the receiver.

'I did, however, enjoy seeing the photostat of the page with my address on it,' I added. 'Look, can I come and see you?'

There was a strained silence, just like the one that his receptionist had employed.

'Mr Eve, I'm very busy with –'

'Guess what I have discovered beneath the floorboards of my house?' I teased.

'When would you like to see me?'

'How about tomorrow?'

'Will this visit be worth it?'

'Oh yes!'

'Tomorrow it is then, shall we say 12.30pm, to allow you time to get here on the train?'

I told him that that was perfect for me, and we hung up. No sooner had I done so, the phone rang. It was Constable Branch, the man who had arrested me the night before. I asked him if he was the policeman that the others often refer to as 'Special Branch'.

'How may I assist you, Mr Eve?' he asked curtly. He'd probably heard it before.

'I need to see you as soon as possible,' I answered. 'I know who killed all those cats and I now have proof.'

'You do, do you?' he said. 'Mr Eve, do you possess an air gun?'

'No,' I replied, lying through my teeth, just in case. My dad's old .177 rifle was in the loft, gathering dust. 'Why?'

'We removed the cats last night to examine them, as you are aware. The police vet confirmed that all eleven of them had been shot with a .22 calibre airgun.'

'Eleven?' I said, shaken. 'I hope she rots in hell for that.'

'Who?' asked Constable Branch.

'Come and see me now if you can,' I said. 'I'll be waiting at home for you.'

Chapter 12

I was extremely early for my appointment with Graham Bateman. So early, in fact, that his previous appointment had not yet been ushered into the presence, and was sitting opposite me in the oak-lined reception area on one of the three comfortable, brown leather settees. He was around thirty, and was wearing a black quilted jacket – The North Face, I think the make was – and new jeans that were pretending to be old - something I don't ever think I will truly understand. He was shortish and sturdy-looking, with short, black hair and a working class London accent. He pronounced water as war'er, think as 'fink' and little as li'oo, and consequently I took an instant, irrational dislike to him. Being a sociable animal, I tried to strike up a conversation nevertheless, and then my irrational dislike became a rational one. He was brash and arrogant, as certain species of London man are prone to being. Cocky Cockney about sums it up. He was seeing Graham about a novel he had written entitled 'The Oblivion Initiative'.

What is it about thriller writers and their titles, I wondered? All their books have names like 'The Equinox Parallel', 'The Betrayal Protocol', or some such bollocks (I made those two up, by the way), and I'm willing to bet you fifty quid that there would be nothing in the story that bore any relationship whatsoever to the silly title. The author, in my opinion, is just gambling on you not even realizing this or questioning it. I loved the film version of 'The Shawshank Redemption', having said that, but now I'm going to have to watch it all again very carefully to see if that title actually had anything to do with the story. I'll let you know Once I've researched it, shall I?

I asked the Cocky Cockney what he did for a living, when he wasn't writing novels, and he said that he was an actor. Well there you go! This confirmed my long-held suspicion that everyone in London, other than the M.P.s, the bankers and the stockbrokers, was a thespian, even if they were so busy waiting on tables that they rarely, if ever, got a chance to actually thesp. Apparently, he'd been in Eastenders (surprise surprise), and he'd also had small parts in Holby City and Casualty - or Holby Ci'ee and Casual'ee, as he pronounced them. I was about to ask what his book was about, when he was summoned upstairs to see the boss. A whole hour later, he walked back into reception and informed me that I was to go up. I thanked him, stood up and promptly fell over, due to the fact that I had somehow succeeded in cutting off all of the circulation to my legs after sitting with them crossed for an hour. The Cocky Cockney said something along the lines of 'Fahkin' mappet!' under his breath and swaggered out into the London sunshine like the missing link, looking mightily pleased with himself. I'd hoped and prayed that his book was shit, and that Mr Bateman had sent him packing with a flea in his ear, but judging by his body language I was considerably wide of the mark.

It was interesting to compare the hospitality techniques of rival publishers. The flash, go-ahead, thrusting young outfit, Capybara, had chosen a dramatic and radical approach, namely, whacking me forcibly about the head with a tea tray as a form of foreplay, before encouraging me to absorb the boiling hot tea through my legs, rather than through my mouth. Edgecliffe's, on the other hand, preferred the more traditional method, whereby a lady who will never see sixty again glides in, as if on castors, avoiding the guest by a wide margin, before placing the tray gently down on the boss's polished wood table and exiting without so much as a word. I helped myself to a biscuit and allowed Graham Bateman to be mother.

Graham, for those traditionalists who appreciate a bit of descriptive work here and there, was a suave, fifty-something who reminded me of Boris Johnson, that Wodehouseian buffoon and Mayor of London, right down to the ridiculous unkempt hairdo that looked as if it had been cut by a council worker in a darkened room with blunted scissors.

I showed him the manuscript and explained how I had come by it. Showing great restraint, he fell just short of drooling. As he pored over it, (as opposed to poured over it, the Capybara way) I informed him that I'd read it from cover to cover, and in my not-so humble opinion, it was a masterpiece. I could almost see the cartoon pound signs forming in his eyes and making that 'ker-ching' cash register noise. What we both found extraordinary was how fortuitous the whole episode had been. If he hadn't sent me that photostat, I wouldn't have known anything about Thomas Bingham. Paul the Plumber would still have handed me the lost manuscript, of course, but it would surely have been tossed in the nearest pedal bin once I'd read the first half a chapter of 'Mary Falls in Love'. Now, we were both potentially sitting on a goldmine. I use the word 'both' in the loosest sense. It might well have been just him.

I took a fortifying sip of tea, coughed a polite cough and asked the question. It was my property after all. Finders keepers and all that. Possession is nine tenths of the law. Graham promised to look into the matter of the estate, surviving relatives and so on, and get back to me. And if the book was anywhere near as good as I had told him it was, Edgecliffe's intended to publish it, and pronto.

I finished my tea, stood up and shook his hand. We agreed to get in touch once he'd actually read the book, and he promised me that I would be 'well looked after', a beautifully non-committal expression.

Having been let down so often in the past, and with the Lost Manuscript Debacle still fresh in my mind, I was in no mood to be counting chickens. Knowing my luck – mostly bad – some disgruntled author, seething as a result of his umpteenth rejection, might return that evening to torch the Edgecliffe's building, and Tom Bingham's old manuscript along with it. I could see the humour in it, nevertheless. An Adam Eve novel lacking a final chapter, and an Adam Eve final chapter tagged onto the end of someone else's novel, both consumed by the flames. Surely, even I couldn't be that unlucky. I eventually allowed myself to be cautiously optimistic, but that was all.

I crawled into my house at around six-thirty, and no sooner had I flopped into my old chair, when the doorbell rang. It was none other than the copper who had arrested me, desirous of a quick word. I invited him in and made him a cup of coffee, and I could tell in an instant that his

114

attitude and body language had changed from that of the previous evening. He had obviously come to grovel and apologize.

'Sometimes, in our game,' he began tentatively, 'we put two and two together, and we just know instinctively that the answer is four, so we don't delve deeper. Unfortunately for us, the answer can - on very rare occasions you understand - actually be three. Or maybe five, if you follow me. Put yourself in my size 12 shoes, Mr Eve. I find the lady's other cat in your house, and then return and find it there again, only this time you're half naked with a weird wig on...'

'Yes, can we skim over that please?' I pleaded.

'...and you've got the cat in your arms and you're threatening to kill it. Then we get a call from the woman over the road saying she's seen you dumping bags full of dead cats... well, you must admit...'

'I understand, honestly I do. If I'd have been you, heaven forbid, I'd have arrested me as well,' I assured him, 'so no hard feelings. What's happened while I've been in London? Any progress?

'Plenty, Adam.'

I was Adam now.

'I went to see the lady, but I didn't mention the CCTV right away. I just said that I needed to ask her a few more questions. She made me take my boots off before I could step on her carpet, and half of her furniture had covers on, to keep it clean. When she offered me a biscuit, and a tiny crumb fell off my plate, I saw her hackles rise, and she immediately suspended the interview at 11.30 a.m. in order to fetch a dustpan and brush. I've seen house-proud types before, but not this bad. She's obviously got that OC/DC, or whatever they call it. Then I asked her if she owned an airgun, and her face turned the colour of a beetroot. She stammered and spluttered a bit, and said, no, of course not.'

'A Kalashnikov, yes, but not an airgun,' I interjected wittily.

'Then I dropped the bombshell,' continued Constable Branch. 'I told her that we'd found the CCTV footage of her, and on hearing this, she fell apart, wailing, sobbing, wringing her hands and so on. I think she's been slowly losing the plot since her husband died. He used to keep the garden just so, she informed me, and hated when neighbour's cats used it as a toilet. Fair enough I suppose. Apparently, he'd once shot one in a fit of pique, years back, and buried it up the garden, after it had killed his beloved tame robin. That's where she got the idea. Every time a cat strayed into her back garden, trying to kill her wild birds or widdling on her plants, she'd load up the old Webley & Scott and take a pot shot at them. Her garden must have been the number one travel destination for all the neighbourhood cats, I have to say. Either that or she's not told me the entire truth. For all I know, she could have been taking the gun out with her in her handbag, and doing them in on the street, under cover of darkness, once the obsession took hold. It wouldn't surprise me. It's a wonder that no one heard the gun going off, not that they make a lot of noise. You'd only have to cough loudly at the strategic time to cover it up. That said, your mate Darrell's in his shed operating his power tools most of the day, or else out on site, and the old chap on the other side's as deaf as a post, so maybe she didn't need to.'

'And did you ask why she chose me to be the scapegoat? I have my own theory, by the way.'

'Yes I did. She seemed to have developed a completely irrational hatred of you, which struck me as odd, but she wouldn't elucidate, other than telling me that she hated your smarmy, superior face - no offence, her words not mine. Did you two have a bit of history then?'

'Yes,' I said, 'but it was nothing, at least, nothing to a rational person, which she obviously wasn't. I caught her, a Neighbourhood Watch person of all people, dropping litter in the street. It seems that her neatness obsession ended at her own front gate. She had the tidiest car in Stourbridge, but only because she emptied her ashtray into the high street, and I had the misfortune, as I now regard it, to spot her at it. The shame of being caught out must have been unbearable, and then ending up living opposite me was surely the last straw. This was revenge, pure and simple. *La vendetta è un piatto che va mangiatto freddo*'.

'You what?' said the policeman, nonplussed. 'You'll have to forgive me. We never did Spanish at school.'

'Er, it's Italian actually. Revenge is a dish best eaten cold. This simmering resentment must have been bubbling away for a couple of years, and then she finally saw a great way to get her own back.'

'Jeez!' sighed the honest copper. 'She's going to just love you now then.

I thanked him profusely for these kind words of encouragement. We stood up at exactly the same time, both sensing that the interview and the apology were concluded, and we shook hands to seal the deal.

117

'Next time,' I gently chided, 'don't go jumping to hasty conclusions. Watch a few episodes of Columbo. It's never the obvious suspect who's done it.'

'Point taken,' the officer replied, 'and if I may offer you some advice too, I would avoid running around the house semi-naked in a ginger wig. It doesn't do you any favours from a suspect's point of view, and from a fashion point of view, it was a bloody disaster.'

'*Touché!*' I admitted, letting him out through the front door. 'I will lock all the doors and close the curtains before I try on my Bay City Rollers outfit tonight.'

Chapter 13

Two Months later

I don't think that I have ever worked so hard in my life. My social life, which was minimal at the best of times, became that of a hermit, or more accurately, a monk that had taken the vow of silence and had locked himself within his cell to illuminate the entire bible. Forgive the digression, but I saw a lovely cartoon about that once. A monk had obviously spent ages beautifully illuminating a large capital letter 'S' with watercolour flowers, gold leaf and filigree work. The abbot pops his head around the cell door and enquires, 'Greetings, Brother Ignatius, How's that Psalm coming on?'

Think about it.

Luckily, I had kept all the plot notes for the novel, and I also found a box file containing some roughly hacked-out, hand-written chapters, which helped a great deal, but having to type the whole thing again was absolute torture. Every sentence that I typed was met with an awful, foreboding sense of unease. Had my original sentence been better than the one I had just constructed? Had I missed out anything that was vital to the plot that was in the original? Was my new Hemingway stripped-down style a bit too sparse? Would Rob read this new version and find it lacked the *je ne sais quois* that the first manuscript had?

I had at long last reached the point, after two months of hard graft and insomnia, where my original novel ground to a halt. Now I had to complete the difficult, final chapter. This time, I had remembered to scrupulously back up my work at regular intervals and copy it to disc – and not one disc, but ten or more. I secreted them all around the house and even left copies at my mother's place. This wasn't just the bog-standard belt and braces approach; it was the Harry Houdini special. Eight belts, three pairs of braces, a load of Velcro and a few ropes and chains for good measure. I was not taking any chances.

My labour of love was running a little late, but I now knew where the final chapter was going, and I was reasonably happy. If Rob was true to his word, he would be on the phone to me any day now. If he rang a little prematurely, before the book was finished, I could at least give him an upbeat report and a firm deadline that hopefully wouldn't cause him to blow a gasket. We were talking a few days, maximum, and even he, stickler that he was, could surely cope with that.

Meanwhile, things had progressed on the Edgecliffe's front too. Graham Bateman had been ringing me on a regular basis about the Bingham novel. As I'd hoped, he too had been knocked out by the quality of the writing, and had moved heaven and earth to bring it to the public's attention in record time, so that he could show it off at the London Book Fair. Proof copies had already been printed and distributed to the newspaper critics, and the initial response had been even more enthusiastic than expected, with some citing the plot as potential Hollywood film material. The Thomas Bingham estate was due a sizeable royalty, as was Edgecliffe's, but it had been unanimously agreed that I was also to profit from the book's publication, to the tune of a healthy 10%. I could no doubt have negotiated more, but I am not a greedy person, and that, in conjunction with my more honestly earned £50,000 advance from Capybara, was quite enough to fund my Waitrose habit, thank you very much. It would also enable me to buy myself a new car, as the old MG seemed to be rotting away in front of my very eyes. Still, they don't build 'em like that any more, as Darrell - who is a vintage car fan - would often inform me, and he is quite right. They build them a damned sight better nowadays.

It was on a Friday, just as I was halfway through my last chapter, that Rob Wakefield eventually rang me.

'Adam, Rob Wakefield,' he said, succinct and business-like as ever. I suspect that, had he chosen to be a copper instead of a publisher, he'd have probably exclaimed 'Thrice hello!' upon disturbing a villain at work, just to save time.

'Ah, Rob, the very man, how are you?' I asked, cordially, for I was feeling pretty much on top of the world and looking down on creation, just like Karen Carpenter used to do before it all went wrong for her.

'Don't fucking 'how are you' me, you slimy bastard!' he replied.

I have to admit that this was not what I was expecting. Call me intuitive and hyper-sensitive if you will, but to my highly trained ear, there was the merest hint of something akin to dissatisfaction in his tone.

'Are you joking with me?' I asked nervously.

'Why would I joke with you, you bottom-feeding little scum-sucker,' he replied. 'How's your depression, you slippery twat? And I thought we were friends! I wouldn't mind, but Edgecliffe's, of all people, our fiercest rivals!'

All of a sudden, I could see where this was heading.

'But Rob, hang on a second, please!' I begged him, 'I need to explain how all this came about. You're being really unfair, ranting on like...'

'Ranting?' he bawled. 'I'll show you fucking ranting, you two-faced, venomous bastard snake in the bloody grass. Howsabout you take that book of yours, and your writer's block, and your bloody depression, and shove them all up your arse without the aid of KY jelly?'

And with that, he was gone.

Words cannot adequately describe how I felt at that point, but as a keen wordsmith I will soldier on and attempt it. I was in a state of severe shock, for a start, like I'd just leaned over an electric fence to stroke a friendly horse, and received an unexpected jolt right through my reproductive equipment, frazzling my prostate. I gawped at the aspidistra plant in the corner of my room for what could easily have been twenty minutes. Then I gawped at the last chapter of my manuscript, which began to swim before my eyes. Eventually, I shifted my glassy gaze to the dead woodlouse that was lying upside down on my window ledge. I knew exactly how he felt. I was desperately trying to fathom out if I had in fact been morally blind, as Rob seemed to be suggesting, albeit in a more earthy way, or if it was he that was being completely and utterly unreasonable. I trawled through the chain of recent events, trying to see them as would an impartial observer. Edgecliffe's was Thomas M.

Bingham's publisher. They had sent me a copy of a letter which had led me to find his manuscript, and I dutifully handed it over to them. To me, that was the right and proper thing to do, and for the life of me, I couldn't see why Rob had taken such extreme exception to the way I'd handled things. After all, it wasn't as if I'd been involved in a secret bidding war over my own novel. I'd promised that to Rob without even checking out the opposition. For all I knew, Edgecliffe's might have offered me twice the advance that he did, but I never even shopped around. Instead, I sold the book to my old friend, and now look how he was repaying me! I needed to ring Rob back and demand that he kept cool and rational while I argued my case. All this ranting and raving was going to solve nothing. I immediately rang the Capybara number and was answered by the young receptionist. I explained to her that Rob had given me a severe dressing down without being cognizant of the facts, and I needed another word. There was a brief silence, while she communicated my message to him, and then she was back on the line.

'I've just spoken to Mr Wakefield,' she said, and he told me to tell you, erm, I er...'

'What did he say?'

'Well, he told me to tell you to go and fuck yourself. I'm ever so sorry, I don't usually use that kind of language, I'm a good Roman Catholic girl, I really am, actually, but he said that if I didn't repeat that exact phrase, he would fire me.'

'That man is a bully,' I growled. 'He has no right to do that to you. Listen, please, please, please, tell him that there's a perfectly reasonable explanation for what's happened, and I need just five minutes, face to face, to explain it properly to him. Tell him I am completely innocent and I have a right to defend myself.'

The lady played me some elevator music while she spoke to him – Greensleeves I think it was, though I wasn't really paying much attention – and a few minutes later she was back on the line again.

'He said you've got five fucking minutes on Monday at 12 noon exactly and it had better be fucking good.'

I thanked her profusely, and suggested that she donate at least a pound to the office swearbox and then say ten Hail Marys.

Chapter 14

To say that I was looking forward to my 12 noon meeting would not be telling the truth. Goats look forward to bumping into tigers on lonely forest paths more than I was looking forward to being in a small office on my own with Rob. As I sat in the Capybara reception area, biting my nails to the knuckle and beyond, I kept asking myself why I was putting myself through this hell. I had spent another £35 that I couldn't afford on train fare, to be sworn at and abused by someone that I had once counted as a friend. I wouldn't mind if I really believed that I could eventually persuade him to change his stance, but somehow I couldn't see it happening. Rob was a great chap, but if he had a fault, it was that he was intransigent. Rhinoceroses are more transigent than he is, if indeed there is such a word.

His personal assistant poked her head around the door and invited me to follow her upstairs. I took a fortifying gulp of air and did as I was told. As I was ushered into the room, I spotted Rob looking out of the window at the mighty Thames River, with his back to me.

'Sit down,' he growled. I gulped again.

He turned around, and his face was like thunder. His assistant asked if I'd like tea, and I was just about to lighten the atmosphere by saying something along the lines of, 'No thanks, not after your last attempt at it,' when Rob cut me short and said, 'He's not having any. Leave us alone.'

She left sharpish. I was thinking of begging her to stay in case there was any physical violence, but I let it go. Besides, she might have sided with her boss if things got out of hand, and started battering me with her silver tea tray again. Rob grabbed a book from his desk and threw it at me.

'Have a look at that first,' he said bluntly.

All of my village cricket training came into play, and I was able to catch the book, thus preventing it from hitting me on the brow. I examined it with forensic precision. It was a thriller-type hardback with the usual, airbrushed, hyper-real book jacket illustration depicting a soldier's hand holding an automatic pistol. Above the illustration was a bold, embossed sans-serif blockbuster title that had a shiny gold drop-shadow. All very yawn-inducing, I have to say - the stuff of airport newsagent shops. What really compounded my dislike of the thing was the title, 'The Oblivion Initiative'.

'What?' I asked.

'Read it.'

'What, all of it? My train's at 5.35.'

He gave me a look that was intended to maim. I opened the book, flicked past the technical bumf and the title page with trembling hand, and found Chapter 1. I began to read it. It was, I have to say, rather good. It was about then that I began to feel very warm, and the room started spinning like a fairground carousel in a Hitchcock film.

Of course it was good. It was my book.

I looked up at Rob, who was looking down at me. If looks could kill, I'd have been at the very least a mass of contusions and hooked up to a saline drip.

'So explain to me how you pretended to be having a bloody breakdown and writer's block and all that bollocks, when all the time you were negotiating a better deal with Edgecliffe's.'

'But, but... but...'

'Ditch the Lambretta impersonation and explain, before I punch your nasty little lights out,' snarled Rob, his face turning crimson.

'Rob, I have never seen this before in my life!'

'Ha ha! Excuse me while I slap my thighs and roar with laughter.'

'On my mother's life, I just don't understand it.'

The back of my neck was ringing wet, and my palms were sticking to the pages. I flicked back and forth feverishly, but for what reason, I had no idea.

'Whose weird notion was the pseudonym and the fake author photo?' asked Rob. 'Gary Butler. Couldn't you have chosen something a bit more catchy? Luca Ferrari maybe?

I flicked to the inside back dust jacket. My God! I knew that face. It was the cocky little bastard that I'd met at Edgecliffe's. He had been peddling *my* book, the brazen sod. My head was swimming now, or at least, it was desperately attempting a life-saving doggy paddle with arm bands on. I really, really wanted to see how the final chapter had ended, but now wasn't the time to be reading a book. I was curious to see what the little shit had cobbled together to finish the thing off.

'But I thought you'd phoned me about Thomas Bingham's undiscovered novel,' I croaked. I desperately needed the cup of tea that had been denied me now.

'What's Thomas Bingham's new book got to do with you?' demanded Rob angrily. 'I couldn't give a shit about Thomas Bingham and his undiscovered novel. I want to know why you sold me down the river. And it had better be good, or I might just break your depressed, scrawny, lying, fucking neck.'

I closed my eyes, as I often did in times of crisis, hoping it would all go away. It didn't. It never did. Then, with one mighty effort, I stood up and confronted him.

'Listen, when I rang you, I asked you to grant me just five minutes to explain myself, and that's what you promised me,' I began. 'So sit down, put those bloody fists away, shut up and listen in silence. Then you can decide if you still want to punch my lights out or apologize. Right, I had an unsolicited letter from Edgecliffe's recently, telling me that my house address had featured in their recent 'Letters of Thomas Bingham' thing. Heard of it?'

Rob nodded moodily. He had seen a press release.

'Just a huge coincidence and nothing more. Turns out his sister used to live in my house. To cut a long story short, my plumber later found a lost Bingham manuscript under my floorboards when he was putting my new central heating system in, so I gave it to Edgecliffe's and they've published it. Any problem so far?'

Rob squeezed his stubbly cheeks together with his right hand, deep in thought. His ice blue stare was like a laser, penetrating my soul.

'That's what I presumed you were livid about, me letting them publish that old manuscript that I'd found. They were Bingham's official publishers since 1939 after all. It was only right and proper. Now, backtrack to the day I met you here for the first time and your P.A. threw tea at me and beaned me with the silver tray. That manuscript was the only printed one I had, remember, and it got ruined so I chucked it. The trouble was, my laptop was stolen on the Euston to Brum train that same night. A pain, yes. Not the end of the world. I went to The Copy Shop – the place that printed that one copy, and asked them to knock out a few more, only the work experience boy had accidentally deleted it. No problem though, they could retrieve it, they said, only then The Copy Shop bloody burnt down. I kid you not. The work experience lad dropped his dog-end in the waste paper basket, they think. Are you seeing a pattern emerging here? So NOW it's the end of the world! Then you ring me asking when it's going to be finished, and in a panic I tell you that I've broken my wrists, to stall you while I try and find my missing laptop. Then you ring again, and I panic some more, and tell you I've got depression and writer's block. I was desperate. It was the first excuse I could think of, in each case. Both rubbish, I know, but I was clinging on to the hope that the police might just retrieve my computer. I asked you for two months' grace, which gave me the time to rewrite the entire book, and just as I'm on the last bloody chapter for the second time around, you ring me again, effing and blinding and telling me to shove my book, amongst other things, up my arse where the sun doesn't shine. And now, to cap it all, this happens.'

Rob continued to rub his cheeks and stare. In fairness to him, it must have taken a long time to let all that lot sink in. After what seemed like five minutes, but was probably only four, he spoke.

'Adam. I apologize. That story just now was so ridiculous, it *had* to be true. You are still a complete twat for not backing up your work and causing us all this mess, but I thought you'd betrayed me, and I now realize that you didn't.'

He proffered his hand and with my own shaking hand, I shook it. He then summoned his P.A. and belatedly asked for tea, while we tried to sort this whole sorry business out.

'The crazy thing is,' he began, pacing up and down with such gusto that I thought he'd wear out the carpet, 'this bloke, this Gary Butler geezer, he's flying by the seat of his pants. Surely he realizes that one day, you're going to come across this book and go mental. For all he knew, it was already published, or if not, about to be.'

'Yes, I agree,' I said, 'but the final chapter was still missing, remember. He probably surmised from that it wasn't ready for publication yet, so he chanced his arm. If it was rejected, all he'd lost is a bit of time spent writing the last chapter. If it was accepted, he stood a chance of gaining a sizeable advance. To his credit, the little bastard, he obviously realized how good the material was. If Edgecliffe's paid him as much as you were willing to pay me, he could disappear with that and leave no forwarding address. It might not even be his real name. Probably not, come to think of it.'

'And what are the chances of you taking your book to the same publisher as him?' asked Rob. 'There are lots of publishing houses in London, so he'd have to have been pretty unlucky to be found out, wouldn't he? It's perfectly feasible that we could publish a book that was being simultaneously published by someone else, in theory anyway, which is a hell of a worry, and something I've never even thought about before now. By the time we cotton on that it's a stolen book, it's too late and we've parted with some or all of the cash. This is why my pep talk about security was so important, remember?'

I winced.

'But who is this bastard?' I said. 'He's not the bloke who stole the laptop, because he was a bald-headed Irishman over at Birmingham International. Presumably, this Gary Butler was the lucky chap in the pub that the Irishman sold it to for twenty quid to fund his next fix.'

'We need to ask Edgecliffe's about him,' said Rob, gesturing for his P.A. to make a very wide arc around my chair with the tea tray. She gave me a sweet smile, and wandered off, no doubt ruminating to herself that men were funny creatures. They could be scrapping in the playground one minute and best friends the next.

'I actually saw the little shit,' I replied. 'In Edgecliffe's reception area. He bragged about being a bit-part actor; said he was in Eastenders and so on. He had short black hair, just a bit longer than it is on that publicity photo, and he spoke with a Cockney accent. He should be very easy to track down, I would have thought, *if* he was telling the truth about the acting roles. The bit I don't get, though, is how he got to see Edgecliffe's without going through a

131

literary agent. I was only able to see you because we knew each other. Aren't they as choosy?'

'More so, if anything,' frowned Rob. 'Maybe *he* had a friend there too.'

'Well, first I need to phone Graham Bateman and explain what's happened,' I said. 'He'll be able to contact this bugger and read him the riot act; have him arrested, whatever. Then comes the awkward bit. They'll have to scrap a load of books and chalk it up to experience. It'll cost them a fortune, no doubt, and there are bound to be red faces all round. Meanwhile, can I take this with me please? I want to see how it concludes. If his ending is better than mine, I'd a good mind to nick it. I also want to compare the original with my new, hopefully improved version. If I've just wasted a whole two months of my life rewriting it for nothing, I will scream so loudly, Edvard Munch will want to paint a picture of me.'

'Poor old Edgecliffe's,' laughed Rob, for the first time in ages. 'First you land them what is sure to be a big money-spinner, and then you take another one off them and hand it back to us. The Lord giveth, and the Lord taketh away.'

We stood up and hugged like long lost brothers, before I said my goodbyes and headed for Euston. I had a strange feeling that things were about to get interesting.

Chapter 15

It was the day after my peacemaking trip to the Capital, and my phone was red-hot. I plucked up the courage and rang Graham Bateman, and it was interesting to observe that I was put straight through. My stocks and shares were at an all-time high following my discovery of the Bingham manuscript, and I was enjoying it while I could. After this call, I was fully expecting my own personal Wall Street Crash.

Graham wished me a good morning, and I reciprocated, but warned him that it may well not be such a good morning once he'd heard me out. I told him the tale in great detail, and he listened, stunned. At one point, I had to check that he was still alive; he'd gone so quiet. I suddenly had a vision of a man slumped in a chair with a purple face and an open, drooling mouth, with words tumbling out of his telephone, unheard, whilst secretaries ran around in a tizzy, like headless chickens with notepads, searching all the drawers for his heart pills.

Like Rob Wakefield, the poor fellow had had a lot to digest at one sitting. Whenever I am involved, it can get like that, I find. Eventually though, he recovered sufficiently to communicate.

'So how on earth did he ever get an appointment without going through a literary agent?' I asked, once he was equal to a spot of conversation. The memory was obviously still green, and I thought I heard him quietly growl.

'Oh! hah! We can blame that on my receptionist,' he said, harrumphing like a retired army major who'd just been informed that the newly appointed Tory M.P. for Tunbridge Wells was a woman. 'This Butler chap turned up unannounced in reception with a manuscript, expecting, rather naively, to be ushered into my office forthwith. She told him that it didn't work like that, and there were procedures and so on. He gave her some old flannel about what a prominent TV star he was, and what an incredible book he'd written, and how it was going to make us a fortune, and if he couldn't get us to read it right away he'd go up the road to Capybara. If I'd have been subjected to that garbage, I'd have slung him out on his arse there and then, but she's more impressionable, being only twenty-three and a bit drippy to boot. She told him that it was impossible to breeze in without an appointment, but after a bit of outrageous flirting, she agreed to read his book on the tube and put a good word in.'

'I see,' I said, smirking at my telephone. The parallels between this tale and my own had not escaped my notice. 'And she reads it, tells you that it's a brilliant piece of work - which it is of course - and you are then tempted to have a nose yourself, just out of curiosity.'

'Exactly. You have it in a nutshell, Adam. I read it from cover to cover and it was, as you so modestly say, quite brilliant, apart from, if I may be so bold, the final chapter, which was strangely clumsy. It seemed rushed, and didn't have the same style of the rest of your book, no offence.

We got a chap in who knows his stuff and he rewrote most of it. I must say, it struck me as odd at the time that this Butler didn't object at all when we suggested it needed looking at. Usually you authors get very prickly if anyone interferes with your work. He just said, 'go ahead. I've struggled with it and written it several times already, so feel free, if you think you can tweak it'. Maybe this should have set the old alarm bells ringing, but hindsight, as they say -'

'Well, I can reveal to you why the final chapter was no good,' I said, with just a hint of Sherlock Holmes about my delivery. 'It's because, when he stole the thing, I hadn't yet written it. Butler had to write that chapter himself, and it sounds as if he made a hash of it.'

'Exactly so,' agreed Graham. 'It takes a lot of skill to take over from another writer like that, and slip into his or her style. I like to think that I can spot it a mile off, after all these years in the business.'

I always thought that this only happened in bad sitcoms, but I choked on my tea at that point, and Paul the Plumber, who had popped by to collect his cheque, had to slap me on the back.

Once order had been restored to its throne, I asked what could be done at that stage. The first priority, said Graham, was to track down this Butler fellow and have him arrested. Edgecliffe's were going to speak to the various TV programmes that he said he'd featured in to see if they had an address for him, as he had rather cleverly 'forgotten' to provide them with one. Apparently, due to the peripatetic lifestyle of the actor, he was more often to be found living in hotels, and he was in the process of selling his small London flat, he'd explained, so communication via the mobile phone was easier all round. Butler had given Graham his number, which he had always answered promptly during negotiations with Edgecliffe's. However, since receiving the first instalment of his considerable advance, Graham's P.A. had been unable to contact him. With nothing to arouse her suspicions at that stage, she had put it down to the usual mobile phone gremlins, coupled with the tendency of some authors and actors to go 'off radar' on occasion, whilst in the middle of some creative urge or other.

It was easy to accuse Edgecliffe's of appalling naïveté, but in their defence, con artists could be very smooth-tongued and convincing. That was how they became con artists in the first place.

I asked Graham what would happen about the printed books, and he replied that everything would have to be shredded immediately, adding that he hoped this could be done quietly, with no embarrassing media attention. I assured him that I would not be ringing up the Daily Mail and saying, 'Guess what?' and neither would Rob Wakefield, even if he really, really longed to. I very foolishly gave him my word that this wouldn't happen.

I thanked Graham for his calm and considered attitude, and said how sorry I was that I couldn't allow him to publish my book; a strategy that would have been the simplest solution all round, especially as Edgecliffe's were apparently offering a £70,000 advance, which was £20,000 more than bloody Capybara offered me. And then, just as we were wrapping things up, Graham mentioned, through gritted teeth, that Gary Butler had been given an initial cheque for £35,000, so he'd presumably decided to take the cash and leg it at that juncture, rather than gamble on securing the rest and getting caught. We weren't sure, of course, if he wouldn't still return for the remainder and get nabbed by burly coppers, but the dead mobile phone was not a good sign. It was around this point when I asked the obvious question.

'Who was the cheque written out to?'

Butler would have to pay it into a bank, would he not? This would be how we could nail him, surely. Graham told me to hang on, and buzzed his accounts lady. A few minutes later he was back on the line, sighing again. The man did a lot of sighing.

'He collected his fee here at the offices. He didn't do it by BACS. He wanted it written out to Wayne Bent, she tells me. He said he was paying it into his dad's account, as he owed him for the deposit on his London flat and that would just about square it.'

'Excellent!' I smiled. 'We are almost certainly looking for a Wayne Bent then. Bent by name, bent by nature, eh?'

A sharper accounts lady might have queried why a man's father had a completely different surname to his son, but I let it pass. Besides, actors did tend to use stage names, so it seemed churlish to criticize her for that. I said goodbye to Graham, and to Paul, who'd loyally hung around just in case I needed the Heimlich manoeuvre again, even though he now had a cheque for three thousand quid in his back pocket. I don't know about you, but I call that good service.

I only had a few thousand words to write in order to complete my book, but, as a result of recent developments, I was a little too hyper and excited to settle down to it. Besides, I wanted to read the Edgecliffe's version before I did that, to see how Graham's in-house man had concluded

137

it. The more I thought about it, having two versions of my own story, and a spare ending to boot, was an embarrassment of riches that I could have done without. Did I go for Version One, ditch it for Version Two, or maybe sift through the whole bloody thing yet again, stealing the best bits from both and ending up with a complete Frankenstein's Monster of a cock-up? Such decisions were quite beyond my limited mental capacity, so instead, I elected to do some detective work.

I did a bit of research on Google, and rang the company that made Eastenders. After being passed from pillar to post, and then back to pillar again (I'll leave out another seven or eight pillars and posts for the sake of brevity) I was told categorically that Gary Butler had never worked on the show in any capacity, and neither had a Wayne Bent.

This was valuable information, painful though it was to source, because a betting man would have deduced from it that if the Eastenders boast was a lie, then probably, so were all the others. However, there is an interesting fact about liars that most criminal psychologists will relate to you, if you ever find yourself down the pub with one, sharing a bag of scratchings. Liars, it would appear, don't often stray too far from the truth when telling lies. In other words, if a man tells you that he played football for England, and it is a lie, there's a very good chance that he did in fact play football, but not at the level he boasted about. It is highly unlikely, however, that he never played at all. What he is doing is embroidering the truth in order to impress, but staying within the boundaries of what he knows about. If one applied the same fundamental principle to the Gary Butler case, it might reveal that, although not a TV actor, he nevertheless had aspirations in that direction. To back up that theory, had he not written his own final chapter, to a competent, if not exceptional standard? It seemed highly likely that our Gary, or Wayne, or whatever his name was, might have been in an amateur dramatics company in the London area. Perhaps that was where I should be searching.

I Googled London area amateur dramatics companies, and wished I hadn't. There were hundreds of them. Most of these outfits didn't have phone numbers that I could ring, and, to be honest, I could recognize a hopeless task when I saw one. I resigned myself to letting Edgecliffe's try and sort it out, packing in the Sherlock Holmes routine and knuckling down to the novel, and yet...

And yet, there was something niggling away in the back of my mind. Some ill-defined, vague, grey, blurred little thought that wouldn't go away. I stared at the wall again and began dreaming. I don't know why, but this often seems to work. It helps focus my mind. On this occasion, however, it didn't.

I picked up the Edgecliffe's printed version of my book, with its ludicrous, completely irrelevant new title, and steeled myself to read the ending. In doing so, my attention was drawn once more to the 'author' photo on the back inner dust jacket flap, and it made my blood boil. I found myself staring long and hard at his annoying face, trying to glean something from it, like a clairvoyant at a séance, and then that teeny-weeny, fuzzy little half idea in my mind suddenly began to come into focus a little. I turned on the TV, grabbed a tape from the nearby rack, slammed it into the machine and pressed rewind. It whirred and chugged for a few minutes before the clunking sound told me it was fully rewound. I pressed play, and was greeted by the familiar title music of Crimewatch UK. I fast-forwarded to the piece about Jeremy's mugging and studied the footage. It was all very dark, as it had been shot in the remotest, uncharted outpost of the Birmingham International car park, from where no explorer has yet returned to tell the tale, but in spite of that, the likeness was uncanny. He was bald and spoke with an Irish accent, but I was nevertheless sure.

The actor in the Crimewatch reconstruction was none other than our old friend, Gary Butler.

Chapter 16

I watched it again and pressed the freeze-frame button. I
held the novel next to my TV, my screwed up my eyes
darting back and forth. I was *sure* that I was right. I
Googled the BBC, found a number, and dialled it. After an
agony of too-ing and fro-ing, I was connected to a nice but
frightfully posh lady called Jennifer. I asked her where the
Crimewatch team got their reconstruction actors from, and
at first, she was reluctant to co-operate, but when I
sketched out my incredible theory for her, she was hooked.
She gave me the number of The Camberwell Agency,
whose tagline on their website was, 'Small Parts are
Beautiful'. They were an agency that specialized in finding
walk-on parts for aspiring actors, and there was a section
you could click on which showed mug shots of the people
on their books. There were several headings, such as Senior
Citizens, Character Faces, Bodies, Breasts, Hands, Foreign
Language Speakers, Ethnic, Teenaged, Middle-Aged,
Eccentric; you name it, it was there. I tried the section
headed 'Men' (20 to 30 years), and scrolled my way
through around fifty lads (that wasn't a euphemism by the
way) until I bloody well found him. Only this time he was
Nick Benton, age 27, lives in Solihull, West Midlands.
Speciality: Accents, Hard Man roles.

Eureka!

So he *was* an aspiring actor after all. I'd been barking up the wrong tree with London. His bloody Cockney accent had fooled me. He lived in Solihull, so he was probably a Brummie, or maybe a Londoner now living in the West Midlands, which explained why he'd been at Birmingham International when he mugged Jeremy. I may have been jumping to conclusions, but surely to God, I was right. There were far too many coincidences. I was a bloody crime-solving genius, and a career in the Met beckoned. I can't tell you how excited I was feeling! It was the Irish accent and the shaved head that had muddied the waters, but simple tricks like that have fooled cleverer folks than me. Do you remember the hunt for Peter Sutcliffe, the so-called Yorkshire Ripper? The police informed us that he had left taped messages to taunt them, just as Jack the Ripper had done, but in written form, and they could therefore reveal that he was a Geordie. This simple statement shifted the entire focus of the operation and wasted a hell of a lot of valuable time. The tapes turned out to be a hoax. Can you imagine, for example, a dragnet being spread all over Europe to catch a criminal with a moustache, with no success? Then, after years of fruitless searching, a new Chief Inspector takes over the case, and comes up with a remarkable new theory. Maybe the fiend had shaved it off.

I rang The Camberwell Agency and asked to speak, in confidence, to the Managing Director, a Mr Keith Watkins, a man, who, despite his many admirable qualities, fine physique and good looks, was destined never to marry. Well, not a woman anyway. I told him that I had some good news, and some bad news. He preferred the good news first, as most people tend to do. I informed him that his agency's casting of a Crimewatch villain had been so spot-on accurate that, as a result of the programme, a man had been identified and would shortly be charged.

The bad news, of course, was that the bloke they'd chosen to play the part of the mugger was also the real-life mugger, which went a long way to explaining why the resemblance was uncanny.

This led an incredulous Keith and me to speculate on the content of the next episode of Crimewatch. Would they now stage a reconstruction of the previous Crimewatch reconstruction, using an actor who looked like the previous actor, but this time wasn't actually him, pretending to mug an actor who looked just like the actor who had played the part of Jeremy? We both agreed that it would be an episode worth watching.

On a more serious note, Keith, after consulting his secretary, Peter, informed me that Nick Benton, alias Wayne Bent, alias Gary Butler, was no longer employed by the agency, because he was unreliable, prone to fits of violent temper, and was almost certainly a crack addict, none of which boded well, especially when one had recently been employed on a programme dedicated to ridding the streets of such specimens. Keith did, however, have an address for the man:

Flat 197, Block 3, Kingsway Estate, Solihull, West Midlands.

The dragnet was closing in.

Now, I don't know about you, but the thing I like best about this police work malarkey is the detecting and deducing part. I'm not quite so keen on the idea of standing in a street wearing riot gear, as building bricks rain down on my helmet, and it is for this precise reason that I felt the next step was to inform the boys in blue. I'd done the hard work, after all, and all they now had to do was go and feel this bleeder's grimy collar. To this end, I rang the local cop shop and asked to talk to my old mate, Constable 'Special' Branch. I thought he'd appreciate being given the opportunity to instigate the arrest of a violent fraudster that had featured on Crimewatch. It would be a huge feather in his cap, metaphorically speaking. A real pheasant feather protruding from his helmet would have made him look a bit foppish, I feel, and he would have been a laughing stock down at the station. Besides, as a reward for one's endeavours, surely a substantial pay rise coupled with promotion would be far more desirable.

I was connected with the officer, who was in the rest room eating a pork pie. I know this because the desk sergeant felt that it was his duty to add this interesting little detail. He probably thought that such descriptive snippets gave the public a fuller picture of what life in the police force was really like.

'Morning, Adam,' said P.C. Branch, through a mouthful of Melton Mowbray's finest. 'Remembered to put your recycling bins out today?'

This, I have to admit, took me into uncharted territory again.

'What?'

'Bottles, tin cans, household waste, newspapers, dead cats...'

'Oh ha ha!' I wailed, once the penny had dropped. 'Been reading your Oscar Wilde books again, have we? Listen, I can do you a major favour here, and it wouldn't surprise me if it led to you becoming an admiral, or whatever it is your top brass coppers are called.'

I gave him the low-down on the Gary Butler situation and he was all ears, and having met him, I mean this both metaphorically and physically. I swear I actually heard the saliva dripping from his mouth and splashing onto the duty desk, at the prospect of being instrumental in arresting such a high-profile suspect. Solihull, he informed me, was not his 'patch', but his opposite number over there would be informed and the flat would be visited by Taser-carrying bruisers as soon as possible. I told him that I would contact the managing director of Edgecliffe's myself and keep him abreast. P.C. Branch congratulated me on my excellent investigative work, and added that there would be a place for me in the C.I.D., if the bottom ever fell out of the writing market. I thanked him brokenly, and asked how the Cat Killer imbroglio was progressing. It was all very sad really, he informed me, once I'd patiently explained what imbroglio meant. Old Curtain Twitcher had seemed genuinely remorseful, he explained, not only about what she'd done, but also for being so vindictive to me. The mists were clearing, and she was beginning to realize that she had been a very silly, not to mention, deranged, old lady. Pride comes before a fall, they say, and she had certainly been on the downright arrogant and morally blind side of the Pride Spectrum for some time. Constable Branch seemed to think that the death of her husband had caused a fuse to blow in her mind, which had resulted in her irrational behaviour. Now she was a broken woman, set to be despised by many, once the news broke. As I said, all very sad, and I was in no mood to gloat. She was currently back at home, on police bail, as I had been, and all she had to look forward to was a court case and the ensuing public ridicule and vitriol. I asked if he still had any contact with her, and he said yes, occasionally. He'd taken it upon himself, like a good beat bobby, to check that she was okay, in spite of hating what she'd done. He didn't want her shoving her head in the gas oven, even if she had murdered half of the neighbourhood moggies. I told him to assure her that I wished her no harm, and that our feud was at an end. One should, I feel, be magnanimous in victory. P.C. Branch promised to do so, and also to keep me abreast of the Solihull situation.

Like all writers, I will do just about anything some days, short of cleaning someone else's lavatory bowl, before I will settle down and write. I'm also one of those obsessive people who like all the loose ends tied, so I felt that I had to contact Jeremy to fill him in on recent events. As you can imagine, it was rather a lot for him to take in, so I left him in peace, in order that he could get his little battered head around it. Then I rang Graham at Edgecliffe's, and finally Rob at Capybara. I have to report that their reaction to my corker of a tale was predictable. They all said pretty much the same thing; that you couldn't make it up, and that truth is indeed stranger than fiction – even the fiction that I write. Can you begin to imagine how the scumbag Butler felt when he got that call from The Camberwell Agency, asking him to play the part of a man who had mugged a commuter, because of his strong resemblance to the villain of the piece? The most delicious irony was, he was now going to get a fee from the BBC for impersonating himself mugging poor old Jeremy, on top of the stolen laptop, wallet, car and publisher's advance. Not bad for a night's work. It reminds me, for some reason, of a supposedly true story about Charlie Chaplin entering a Charlie Chaplin Lookalike Contest and coming a poor third.

Chores completed, I sat down at my desk, turned on my new laptop and opened up the file marked 'Book Rewrite'. Graham had kindly provided me with a disc of the Butler version, which I'd saved. I opened that too, and began the laborious task of flitting between the two and comparing them.

After half an hour of this, I had developed the mother of all headaches and I was totally befuddled. Have you ever tried to read two slightly different 70,000 word versions of the same story simultaneously, while trying to determine which bit of which sentence is better? Well of course you haven't, but you can see what I'm getting at. After ten minutes I no longer had a clue which version was which, and I was delirious. It was then that I made an executive decision, based on the following logic:

Rob had read Version 1 and loved it. Rob had not read Version 2. If it is not broken, do not fix it.

I deleted all of the 70,000 words that I had just spent two whole months rewriting, after of course checking at least fifteen times to make sure I was getting rid of the right version. With my recent track record, you couldn't be too careful. In one nervy click of a switch, executed while offering a silent prayer to a God I always insist I don't believe in, they were history. Now all I had to do was sort out the ending. I scrolled to the final chapter and read it. It was...well, alright I suppose, but nothing like the scenario I'd roughed out for my own version, and besides, it was tainted, if you know what I mean. I deleted it and set about creating my own last chapter.

By six p.m. on the following day, the final sentence of my novel was at last completed. I had written and rewritten it at least twenty times, and I was now satisfied that it was perfect. I was more than satisfied – I was downright ecstatic, but my exhilaration very quickly turned to utter exhaustion and I flopped back lifelessly into the depths of the settee, staring into space, too tired to move. Even my laptop seemed to breathe a sigh of relief. The small concluding sentence I was now mindlessly gawping at was the culmination of a whole year of blood, sweat and tears, and the mental relief of finishing it had suddenly reduced me to dried husk, a hollow shell and a spent force in the order named; a bit like one of those charred sky rocket carcasses you find poking out of your Rhododendron bush on November 6th.

Isn't that odd? I just had one of those spooky *Deja Vu* moments then, like I'd typed that exact paragraph before. Do you ever get that?

Anyway, outside, it was a typical, English Summer's day, by which I mean, it was grey, cold and drizzling with rain. It was late June, for God's sake, but it looked and felt more like January. Apparently it was the Jet Stream's fault, whatever that is. Usually it hangs around well to the north of Scotland, but recently it had relocated to England. Perhaps it was sick of all the rain in the Highlands and fancied a holiday, I don't know.

All of a sudden, I began to shiver. I dragged myself off the settee and decided to switch the new central heating system to manual to warm the place up a bit. I clumped upstairs, located the switch with the aid of the instruction manual, (it was all still new to me, and would always be) and clicked it down. At this point, it was supposed to make a noise like a wildebeest farting under water and then start humming. It didn't. I checked the booklet, just in case I'd accidentally switched everything off by mistake, but no, I'd done it properly, miraculously. Something, it appeared, had gone awry. I experimented with flicking the system back to automatic and moving the timer forward, so that the boiler was fooled into thinking it was time to turn itself on.

Nothing.

It was time to ring Paul the Plumber, superhero. Paul talked me through several exercises with no success, so he said he'd come out to see what was the matter, but before he could come, there was the small matter of his dinner, which, for those who take note of these things, was lasagne (his favourite). He promised to be at my place by 7.30pm, so I told him that I was going to The Princess just down the road, meanwhile. I fancied a celebratory glass of Shiraz, (much nicer than a cupful) now that my book was completed, and I knew Darrell would be there, he being a creature of habit (namely, a drink habit). He might have been the World's Most Boring Teller of Anecdotes, but he was fundamentally a nice chap, liked to play pool and so did I, and besides, I could usually paste him when he'd had one too many. Last but not least, it was probably considerably warmer in The Princess than it was in my house. I grabbed my big coat and my cricket club cap, selotaped a hastily scribbled note on my door saying 'Back at 7.30pm' and then braved the elements, muttering to no one in particular, 'I'm going out now, and I may be some time,' as I slammed the door shut. I noticed Curtain Twitcher at the window, and as a conciliatory gesture, I gave her a half wave, which she reciprocated, and not with a two-fingered salute either. Maybe P.C. Branch had had a quiet word already.

Darrell was there, as I had predicted, boring the landlord rigid with one of his meandering tales. From what I could glean, the main thrust of it was that he intended, from that evening onwards, to hide his wallet in the cooker, because his wife would never find it there. Not a bad joke, as it happens, had it been judiciously pruned by around twenty minutes. We played a few frames and I am happy to report that the carpenter was soundly thrashed by the writer; so soundly, in fact, that he hung up his cue and called it a day. I could feel another 'No, only...' coming on at that point, so I made my excuses and legged it down the road to let Paul in.

It was freezing now, and the rainy skies had made it prematurely dark, like a winter's evening, though it was still only twenty past seven. I let myself in, closed the door and hung up my coat, when the front door bell chimed. I opened the door again to let Paul in, but it wasn't Paul. At least, not unless he'd shrunk by six inches, run the clippers over his hair since I last saw him, and developed a taste for carving knives. What happened next was something of a blur. I was aware of being slammed backwards into the hallway with the force of a steam train, causing me to crack my head on the stair post. Gary Butler, or whatever his name was, was right in my face now, his one hand clamped onto my hair, yanking at it till I thought it would all come off in his clenched fist. I saw the flash of the blade and I felt a sharp stabbing pain in my cheek. His bulging, manic eyes were inches from mine, and there was spittle at the corners of his snarling mouth.

'You fucking twat!' he growled, as he shook my head back and forth, digging the knife further into my cheek till I began to yelp like Bill Sikes's dog after a good kicking. I felt utterly helpless, in pain and frightened rigid. If I tried to struggle the knife dug in more. I was a very reluctant captive audience.

'I've had the Old Bill around my flat,' he snarled. 'I had to piss off sharpish through the back window and hide in a fucking skip. I came within seconds of losing my thirty-five grand and my freedom, all because of you, you arsehole.'

'What do you mean, me?' I asked, or at least, that was what I was trying to say. My lip was trembling so much, I could barely form the words.

'You found out where I lived from the agency, didn't you, you wanker? I heard the copper tell his mate while I was hiding in that stinking skip, covered in stale, foul-smelling Indian shit from the takeaway next door.'

I was wondering what he smelled of. Isn't it funny how, even in times of severe stress, our minds can still be quite rational?

'What do you want from me?' I begged. 'That knife is cutting me, I'm bleeding all over the place. Please, there's no need for this.'

'What do I fucking want, you say? I'll tell you what I want.'

He raised the carving knife high in the air. There was a flash of metal, and I shut my eyes, and in that split second, I seemed to be processing around a hundred thoughts simultaneously. This must be what they mean when they say that your life flashes before your eyes. It really did, and my life's been so disappointing, let me tell you, that I didn't really want to go through it all again. I thought how unjust it was that it was to be so unceremoniously ended, with no time to see my mother, my kids, my ex-wife, Katie, my brother and sister. All this, if you can believe it, within an instant. But no blow came. And yet I heard it; heard the

151

sickening thud, the dull groan. I opened my eyes, and saw Butler staggering backwards, blood all over his face, his once manic eyes now resembling those of a dead halibut on a fishmonger's slab.

Then I heard a voice. Ethereal, surround-sound. Behind me maybe. Hard to say.

'Adam, Adam, are you okay?'

I turned around, in a slow motion daze, as if I were deep under water. Paul. Paul the Plumber. Holding his claw hammer. Looking paler than an albino ghost with anaemia. Maybe he *was* a ghost. Maybe we both were.

And then the doorbell rang. We looked at each other and then at it, if it's possible to look at a sound. I tumbled over Butler's lifeless body, picked myself up somehow and opened it with shaking hand. I caught my reflection in the hall mirror. Blood was trickling from a hole in my cheek and all over my new shirt. Another bloody shirt bloody ruined, I thought. I love wordplay, me, even in times of stress.

It was P.C. Branch. He was special. Special Branch. Always there when you needed him. Always there when you didn't. Ears like the F.A. Cup.

'Adam, are you okay? Answer me. Any knife wounds?'

'I'm, erm, almost fine, I think, apart from this,' I stammered, lightly fingering my cheek and examining the blood on my first three fingers. 'Don't know about Butler though. He doesn't look well does he? Don't know why. Couldn't have hurt that much, the big baby. That hammer was only on his head for a second!'

I opened the door as far as it would go, which wasn't too far, as Butler was blocking its progress. Butler the draught excluder. The policeman came in, stepped over the body, itching, no doubt, to trace round it with a stick of chalk. He was followed by Curtain Twitcher, biting her nails, fragile-looking, curiously rodent-like. P.C. Branch bent down to examine Butler, whilst simultaneously probing me about what had happened. He cuffed him with consummate skill, quick as a flash, and then coaxed the trembling plumber down the stairs and thanked him on behalf of all of us. He had almost certainly saved my life with his accurate hammer work. If the bottom fell out of the plumbing market, he had a bright future ahead of him at the Highland Games. I'd have thanked him myself, but my mouth didn't seem to want to work. Then I suddenly felt hot. Maybe Paul had managed to mend the central heating system. That was quick! My vision closed in, and I went limp. I fell to earth I know not where.

Chapter 17

One Week Later

P.C. Branch had popped by for a cup of tea, and to see if I was okay, now that I had had a bit of time to recuperate. I was; I even had an 18th Century duelling scar, which I'd always wanted. I introduced him to Katie and the kids, who'd also dropped in to say hello. Apparently, so he informed me, after I fainted, it was carnage. All hell broke loose. I'm glad I wasn't there to witness it really. In my cramped hallway, I had managed to faint and then fall on top of Butler. Branch and The Curtain Twitcher had come in, but couldn't find anywhere decent to stand due to the unusual number of unconscious people cluttering up the hall floor. Then, bang on cue, Paul the Plumber, who was convinced that he had killed his first man, decided to faint as well. He slithered down the stairs on his arse, his head rapping each step as he descended, and joined the ever-growing pile at the bottom. Darrell, en-route for home from The Princess, had seen and heard the commotion and waded in to investigate, but was being told in no uncertain terms by P.C. Branch to back off and allow him some room. Then Barbara from next door arrived, offering to make tea, closely followed by two ambulance men and two more coppers with a vicious-looking Alsatian called Wilson.

By the time I was *compos mentis* again, they'd carted Butler off in a van, which was a relief. If I never saw his vile fizzog ever again, it would have been ten years too soon for me. I learnt that it was Curtain Twitcher who had called the police, which was her act of redemption in a way. (Which reminds me; Shawshank was the name of the prison. Fair enough I suppose, but I still hate those silly book titles.)

She'd seen a strange man hanging around my front garden, wearing a black duffel coat and secreting what looked, through her binoculars, like a kitchen knife. She could easily have been treated like the boy who cried wolf after her 'dead cats in the bin bag' phone call, but to his credit, P.C. Branch felt that it was his duty to investigate, and being as he was one street away at the time of the call, castigating a youth for lobbing a Special Brew can into a pensioner's garden, he was able to get to the scene of the crime in record time. Paul, it turns out, still had the key that I had lent him, and finding the master not at home, had let himself in and got started, because there was a crime drama he wanted to watch at nine on BBC2. Sadly, due to one thing and another, he never got to see it. Not to worry, they repeat these things nowadays if they're any good, and if not there's always i-Player. Besides, who needs the TV when you've been in a real-life crime drama of your own?

Butler, sadly, survived, albeit with a fractured skull, and was facing a hell of a long time in jail. He had with him, in yet another stolen car, a bag full of money, which the police were returning to Graham Bateman in due course, but a search of his seedy flat failed to find my old laptop or

155

Jeremy's car keys and wallet. It did uncover a sizeable stash of crack cocaine though, so Keith Watkins had been correct about that.

P.C. Branch finished his tea and stood up, ready to go. We hovered around each other and were on the verge of a manly hug, but in the end we settled on a firm handshake. I thanked him profusely, and said that he was welcome, any time he was passing by on his beat, to drop in for tea and biscuits.

'You know, 'he smiled, 'we should have known it was him all along. We missed one big, vital clue. Columbo wouldn't have missed it, I bet!'

'What was that?' I asked.

'Well, it's always the Butler that did it. We should have realized.'

'Jeez!' I winced. 'You've opened your Christmas crackers early this year.'

The P.C. admitted that he'd been polishing that line up all day, and was rather proud of it, in spite of my derogatory comment.

'Oh, before you go,' I said, 'are you heading anywhere near Bridle Road?'

'I could be, why?' he asked.

I popped into the kitchen and returned with two beautiful tortoiseshell kittens in my arms. Katie, Lauren and James clasped their hands to their mouths and said 'Aaaaaah!' in unison.

'I took the liberty of purchasing these little fellows from a mate of mine, whose cat has become a mother of six. I'm going to keep this one, because life's been a bit lonely since my dog Len died, bless him, and I wondered if you'd like to deliver the other to the lady who lost Puddles. There's no obligation. If she doesn't want him, I'll keep the two. I'm not bragging or anything, but I can afford two cats now that my book advance has arrived and the Edgecliffe's one is on the way!'

'That's very decent of you, Adam,' said the good officer. 'I'll do that very thing right away.'

'Hang about!' I added. 'I bought two cute collars for them, with little discs so she can have its name engraved. I daresay she'll want to call this one Tinkle or something. Wait there!'

I went to the cloak room in the hallway and fiddled around in my old Barbour dog-walking coat, looking for the cat collars. I dug them out, and then found something else in the dusty corner of the left waist pocket. It felt like a disposable lighter, which was odd, because I don't smoke. I fished it out and examined it. It was a small black USB memory stick. I stared at it in blank disbelief for a good minute, until P.C. Branch broke the spell by calling to see if I was okay.

'Oh yes,' I laughed. 'I'm, erm, fine, thank you. Just a touch of memory loss, that's all!'

THE END